Dedicated to my first love.

One More Race

Book Playlist

Born to be Wild by Steppenwolf

Would you go with me by Josh Turner

Your Love by The Outfield

The Joker by Steve Miller Band

Why don't we just dance by Josh Turner

Every breath you take by The Police

More than a feeling by Boston

Feels like the first time by Foreigner

Your Man by Josh Turner

Alycia Carosella

Prologue

"Can you hand me the socket wrench right there?" I grab the wrench out of the toolbox and hand it to my father. Even though it isn't race season, we work on the race car year-round. It gives us something to do and gets us excited for summer. Race season just ended, and I start school in a few weeks, unfortunately. I'm not sure what we are doing to the car right now, but I like to be in the garage working on something.

I get a lot of backlashes from other kids my age for being interested in a "man's sport," but I just ignore them. Who said a girl can't race anyways? I mean, Danica Patrick races and she is rather good at it! She races Nascar and I much prefer dirt races, but it's still racing. I can't wait for

One More Race

the day to come when I can get into my own race car on the track.

"Are you excited to start school and see all your friends again?"

I sigh when my dad asks about school. He thinks I have loads of friends that I'm so desperately missing all summer long. To be honest, I don't really have any friends at my school. They don't understand my interests and it's boring not being able to talk about cars. Jackson and Andy are my real friends, but they both go to a different school. I only get to see them on the weekends sometimes and during the summer at the speedway. I decide to lie and make it seem like school is so great and I'm loving it.

"Yeah, I can't wait for next year and to finally be in high school!"

Alycia Carosella

I can see my dad look at me with pride but also sadness in his eyes. He gets like that when I remind him how I'm getting older. He thinks I won't be his little girl anymore. He can think whatever he wants as long as he keeps his promise and lets me race this coming summer.

One More Race

Taylor

I swear this has been the longest fifteen minutes of my life! I've been staring out the window and back at the clock for the past half hour waiting for the bell to ring. This is the last class before summer is official here. This year flew by and to be honest I don't even remember most of it. I kept my head down for most of it and just focused on my schoolwork. The same I do every year to make it through. The way I see it is if I do good in class then I pass and that's one more year down that gets me closer to graduation. It's not that I don't like school, I just want to be able to do what I want to do and not sit in a classroom learning boring lessons.

I take another glance at the clock, and I swear the time hasn't changed at all. I have no idea what our teacher is even talking about. I've been so zoned out since the class started; I feel like I'm not even here. I grab my phone out of my pocket and send a message to Andy and Jackson. We have a group message that we all use to see if we are all going to the races and where we are going to meet up. Most of the time we are in the pits helping so it's not hard to find each other.

Taylor: Hey you boys ready for the races in a few weeks?

Jackson: I'm pretty sure we have been ready since the school year started! The race car has been ready since we pulled her in the trailer last year. Has your dad been working on the car still?

Jackson's dad and my dad both race big blocks together and that is what brought Jackson into my life. Well, I guess it's what brought me into his since he is a year older than I am.

Andy: Heck yes! They are starting the go-kart track the week before the big track. Will you go to watch me?

Andy has been friends with us for a couple of years now and he fits right in. We are like the three peas in a pod when we are together. These guys are my best friends, even when I get a bit jealous of them for not getting backlash about wanting to race. Andy got his go-kart last year and started to race a bit last summer, but this year will be his first actual full race season. Jackson and I both have been waiting to get a go-kart so we can all race together, but I haven't been able to convince my parents yet to let me.

Jackson: Of course, but you might have some competition out on the track this year!

Jackson sends a picture of a go-kart, it's not much but it's a start. Andy's dad bought his brand new but for Jackson and me, our families come from the middle class, so we buy used and fix it up ourselves. I don't hold it against Andy at all though, we can't control what kind of family we are born into.

Taylor: You finally got one? Damn looks like I have some work cut out for me.

Andy: can't wait to see what it looks like once you've finished it. It'll be so much fun to race with

One More Race

each other. You'll have to be on two pit teams now Tay!

I hate that Andy thinks it's funny to poke at me about being the pit team all the time. I know he is just kidding but I would be lying if I said it didn't bother me. I want to be on the track with the boys, but being a girl makes it so much more difficult. When I tried to convince my parents to get me a go kart, they kept pushing it off another year.

    My dad always says that racing is a dangerous sport and that my mother wants to wait as long as she can before getting me behind the wheel. I can see in his eyes that the reason is his too. He is scared that I'll wreck and get hurt. It's a totally justified reason, but that is the risk of this sport. My mother always reminds me of how girls my age is dating and going out to movies and shopping. Sometimes I feel like she doesn't understand me at all. She supports my father and allows me to be part of that, but she would rather have me do "girl things" just like everyone else does.

Great, I'm in a shit mood and this damn bell still hasn't rung yet. I put my phone in my pocket and waited the extra few minutes of class. The bell finally rings, and all the kids are packing their bags and running out to their buses to start their summer. I'm doing the same and as I'm walking out of the classroom, I feel my phone vibrate again. I pull it out and it's a text from Jackson.

One More Race

Jackson

I hate when Andy says shit like that to Taylor, I know he is joking but he should know that it hurts her feelings too. I send her a private text out of the group chat to make sure she is all right; I know she really wants to be the one behind the wheel and not the one just working on the cars. She has talked about it for as long as I can remember. I admire her for having that goal and sticking to her guns to try to make it happen.

Jackson: Ignore him, he just doesn't want you on the track to beat his ass lol

Taylor: Thanks Jack, what you going to do when I beat your ass too though.

    I smile at her response; I would let her win any race against me if it would make her happy. She would be pissed if she knew that I let her have it easy, but I love to see that smile on her face. The little creases it makes near the corner of her hazel eyes, the gaps in the front of her teeth that show when she actually smiles showing her teeth. She's so self-conscious about her smile because she is missing those two teeth, but I think it makes her smile unique and hers.

    I know we are supposed to be just friends, but I have memorized her in my head. Like she is permanently seared into my brain as the only person

One More Race

I want for the rest of my life. Just thinking about those long lashes that accentuate her eyes, all the freckles on the bridge of her nose and her cheeks that get more noticeable in the sun, her sunshine blonde hair that falls just above her shoulders, her gapped tooth smile, the way she always smells like flowers. I wish she knew how beautiful she was and didn't doubt herself, but I will always be here by her side reassuring her that she is enough and to push her to her goals. It's my job after all...being the best friend!

Jackson: We will see if you put your money where your mouth is when you're on the track with me this summer!

Taylor: I kind of need a race car to race you lol

Alycia Carosella

Jackson: you'll get one, your dad promised that he would get it for you the summer before high school. Now is the time, don't let him forget it! Garage tonight?

Taylor: Absolutely! Andy is going to come over too. I'll see you later Jack

Jackson: see you later Tay

Andy always comes around now, and I would be lying if I said it didn't annoy me. Tay and I have been friends longer than he has been in the picture and sometimes I sense that he likes her, and I get extremely jealous. I don't want him to be her guy, that's my job! I wish I could tell her how I feel for her, but I don't know if the feelings are the same on her side and I don't want to jeopardize our

One More Race

friendship over it. So, I'll wait, I mean we are only teenagers, we have the rest of our lives ahead of us.

When I get home the cars are already packed into the hauler and my dad is packing the tools into the truck. When summer starts, we bring the car, we'll technically cars now that I have my go-kart over to Taylor's dad's garage. Sam's garage is bigger than the one car garage we have here so it's easier to put all the cars inside one area when we work on them. I can't wait to see Taylor in person, but I'm also apprehensive a bit about bringing my go-kart. I don't want to make her feel sad about being the only one there without a race car.
"Can we leave my car here for now? We will probably not work on it much tonight anyways?" I can see my dad slowly turn towards me and raise his eyebrows.

"Are you sure that's the only reason you don't want to bring it?" I see a little smirk forming on his face and I want to slap it off his face.

"Yes, that's the only reason, why else would I ask?" I already know what he is going to say but I ask anyway.

"Oh, I don't know, maybe you don't want to bring it because that means Taylor will be the only one there without a car and you want to make sure your girl isn't sad?"

He puts his hands on his hips and leans a bit forward like he nailed it right on the head. He did but I'm not going to let him know that.

"First off, stop doing that with your hands, it makes you look like a soccer mom about to yell at their kid. Second, Taylor isn't my girl, we are just friends!"

One More Race

He doesn't move his hands from his hips, so I mock him by doing the same. He starts to laugh and nudges me with his shoulder while walking toward the house.

"Don't act like you haven't been in love with that girl since the moment you laid eyes on her." I turn toward him and follow him into the house totally ignoring his remark. We finish getting ready and head out toward Taylor's house.

Alycia Carosella

Taylor

When I get off the bus my dad and mom are outside the garage talking, but as soon as they see the bus, they stop. I see them both turn towards me, my mom looks agitated, but my dad looks excited. I give them a smile and start towards them to try to figure out what they were talking about. My mom's face starts to soften the closer I get to the garage. "Hi honey, how was your last day?" My mom is trying to make conversation but it's weird that we are doing this outside. She is usually inside either cleaning or getting dinner ready. She supports my dad's love for racing, but she rarely goes into the garage. She watches him but not as much as she used to, she only really goes when I have to sit in the stands rather than be in the pits. I think she thinks too much about the crashes that could happen. I don't blame her though; I would lose it if someone I loved had crashed their car on the track and got hurt.

"It was good, what's going on?"

I see them both glance at each other and my dad answers me first.

"We have a surprise for you!" I can see the excitement on his face, and I know they both can see the excitement on mine as well. It's starting to hurt from smiling so much, I can't believe it's finally here, that he kept to his promise.

Alycia Carosella

He opens the garage door and there is an old go kart sitting on a stand in the front of the garage. The body is in bad shape, but we can fix that. If the frame is good, and we have an engine then the rest we can do ourselves. I can already picture what it's going to look like once I'm finished with it. I feel wetness on my face, and I know that I am crying now, not sad tears, happy tears. I turn and run to my parents and hug them both so tight I swear they can't breathe. I have never been so excited in my life for anything!

"Thank you, thank you, thank you!" I feel the hug tighten with my mother's hold which is surprising. I know she didn't want me to race but it's nice to know that she was part of this and is willing to give it a try.

One More Race

"It needs some work, but we have time to get it ready before the first race."

"It's perfect, I can't wait to get started on it! I love you guys so much!" I kiss them both and follow them into the house to drop off my backpack. I'm drawing ideas for what I want my body to look like when I'm done painting it when I hear my dad yell that Andy is here. Before I can answer he is in the doorway of my room asking what I'm doing.

I wave to him to sit down next to me and show him what I've been working on. His eyes grow wider when he sees it.

"That's awesome Taylor, you should paint bodies for a living. You would make so much money from it." I roll my eyes and laugh at him.

"It's for my own kart you goon!" His smile grows so big with my response.

"You finally got your car? Omg that's awesome Taylor!"

He gets up and gives me a hug, that's when I notice Jackson in my doorway. He looks a bit sad or angry at what he is seeing, no it's not that, he looks jealous. I caught him being like that sometimes, but I think it's just because it used to be just us for the longest time and then poof, Andy came into our friend group.

Boys are weird sometimes when it comes to friendship, they are too territorial when it comes to who is closer with who. I am grateful that I have them both as friends though, without them I would have no one. I think that is why my mother allows them in here, she knows we are just friends and that things won't happen. I mean two teenage boys in

One More Race

my bedroom sounds like a teenage girls dream but

to me it's just my best boys hanging out.

Alycia Carosella

Jackson

As soon as we got to Tay's house, I went straight to the house instead of unloading first. I wanted to see her, I wanted to see her freckled face and those eyes. I hate what I walked into, seeing them hug made me want to vomit. My stomach churned at the sight of his arms around her and her reciprocating the hug. I know that sounds dramatic, but I don't want him getting any ideas, just friends, that's all they are. It's hard having another guy in our friend mix and having to share her with him.

She isn't mine but sometimes I act like she is, and I need to get it under control. She doesn't need me to protect her, she is her own person and is more than capable of taking care of herself. I just can't help myself sometimes, I always worry about her and want to make sure she is safe and most of all happy. I just stand there for a little because I'm not sure how to break the awkwardness I just created for myself.

That's when she notices me standing there and we lock eyes. I could look into those hazel eyes for eternity and never get bored. Her eyes have a little of every color in them, in the sun they have more green than brown and at night they are browner, but she has a little bit of blue lining the outside of her irises. It is fascinating seeing how they change but still make me feel the same every time. She looks away first and stops hugging Andy. She makes her way to me and wraps her arms around me next and I freeze for a second. It's not the first time we have hugged but my thoughts of her have me stunned in place. She comes up to my ear and whispers. "Guess what I got today?" Her question brings me back to reality even though I'm engulfed in her flower scent and just want to stay like this forever. Wrapped around her, wrapped in her scent looking down at her blonde hair.

"Your go-kart would be the perfect answer for that." I don't say it definitely because I don't want to make her feel bad if she didn't in fact get it yet like her dad promised. That's when she looks up at my face and she smiles, like, really smiles. I see the happiness in her eyes, and I swear I forget how to breathe.

"Yes!" She is jumping up and down and twirling around in her room now and I can't help but chuckle. Andy is doing the same because she never is this happy, of course she gets excited at the track, but I can see a flick of sadness when she is there too; when she realizes she isn't the one behind the wheel. She truly was born to race, and I love that, I think that is one of the reasons why I love her so much. *Wait, did I just think that? Love? Do I love Taylor?* I shake my head to try to come back to the present and not get lost in my thoughts. I'm going to be a sophomore this year, I don't know what love is yet.

"Come on guys, I want to show it to you!" She grabs my hand and Andy's hand and leads us to the garage.

When she is standing next to her car, I can see the excitement in her the way she is standing and looking at the old kart. It reminds me of mine a bit, we both grew up with parents who worked for what they wanted. That means we didn't always get the new shiny things. We got used things that we put work into and made it our own. Some would be embarrassed of that, but I can tell she isn't in the slightest.

"Isn't she beautiful?"

"It needs some work, but I have no doubt you will make it look as beautiful as the driver." Andy smiles after that remark but all I do is keep my eyes on Tay to see how she reacts to him. I want to say something better just to one up him, but he is our friend, and I don't think he meant anything by it. Taylor must think he did because she is blushing now and looking down at her shoes like she's all timid out of nowhere. I hate that he just did that to her.

"Are you trying to sweeten up your competition so she will still let you win?" I nudge his shoulder and laugh. He gives me a smile back and Taylor is laughing. God her laugh is the most beautiful sound. I always thought a car engine was music to my ears until I heard her laugh for the first time. Then Taylor was music to my ears, and I just can't get enough!

Alycia Carosella

Taylor

I was flattered when Andy called me beautiful, it's nice to know that someone does think I look good. Being tough all the time is exhausting, but I must act tough to not show my insecurities. Even though we are a close-knit group I wouldn't be lying if I said Andy was attractive, he has the dark brown hair that is a bit longer than his ears. It sweeps just over his chestnut brown eyes, and he is very tall, well more like gangly because he is super skinny too. He

One More Race

has this nerdy, skater vibe going for him, and I don't really have a type to be honest. I don't really think about relationships like that, in the romantic sense. I mean I'm only a teenager, so I have some time before committing to someone fully.

I am starting high school this year so having a boyfriend wouldn't be too out of the ordinary. I mean if I even wanted to entertain that idea with Jackson. *Wait I meant Andy, not Jackson!* My brain gets messed up sometimes when I'm around both. They are both particularly good looking and they are great friends. They both make me feel good in separate ways. I've known Jackson longer than Andy and they look so different. Jackson has a bigger build and sandy blonde hair just like me. Well, mine is significantly lighter than his but his eyes. I can't get enough of them; they are a dark blue like an ocean. Every time I look into them, I feel like the world disappears and I'm floating in his ocean eyes. They truly are beautiful just like his muscular build and his crooked smile. He got blessed with straight teeth unlike me, but his smile is crooked.

When I first saw him smile, I thought it was so cute and unique the way one side went up and the other side looked like it was smirking. He always smells like the garage too and it makes me feel like I'm home when I'm around him. Maybe that's how it feels when you love someone, like your home when they are around you? But I don't think Jackson feels like that with me. He never makes moves like Andy does.

When Jackson makes the remark about me letting Andy win it makes me laugh because I would never let the boys win and I would hope that they would never let up on me either. A fair race is when you put your all into it.

"I will never let you boys just win, I'll always put my all into every race. And I expect you to do the same."

They both nod and smile at me which makes my knees weak. I don't know why suddenly I'm feeling this way towards them. Hormones, it must be hormones! We get everything unloaded and organized into the garage and then get to stripping all the cars. Andy's car is back at his house, so he helps with our karts for the night. We lose track of time while we are in the garage.

"My dad is here to pick me up, I'll see you guys Sunday at the racing expo, right?"

Jackson and I both nod because we know our dads are going to be there regardless. I walk to Andy and give him a hug.

"Thank you for your help today. Goodnight Andy" I smile at him to show my appreciation for his remark earlier.

"It's no problem, Taylor, I'll always be here to help you. Goodnight"

    He grabs my arms and kisses me on my cheek. I don't flinch but I don't move either because I've never been kissed before. I mean I've never been anything before now, I know it's not a real kiss, but it's still something. He turns around and smirks at me with a nod of his head towards Jackson. I'm still in shock at what just happened and I'm just glad that my dad didn't see what happened because he would probably have talked

One More Race

about how I'm not allowed to date until I'm thirty. I'm knocked back to reality with a loud crash of what sounds like a wrench getting thrown to the ground. I turn to see Jackson walking outside near our fire pit area. I mean it's almost 7:30 now so it wouldn't be a bad idea to start one, but we were just in the middle of putting things semi back together.

Alycia Carosella

Jackson

What a smudge little asshole! I can't believe he just kissed her, well technically on the cheek isn't a real kiss but it's still affection I didn't want to see. I must get some air before I freak out. I usually can keep my cool around Taylor but lately Andy has been showing more interest in her and it seems like she is reciprocating it. Maybe that is who she wants, and I should let it happen, who am I kidding, it will happen regardless of what I do because Taylor is her own person, and she deserves to be happy. If

One More Race

Andy makes her happy then I will support, her decision even though I know I will make her happier.

I hear her footsteps following me outside to the fire pit and I don't know if I should be excited or worried. She definitely heard me throw the wrench, but I don't want her to think I'm mad at her. I grab logs and start stacking them in the pit to get a fire started. I turn to her standing just staring at me, the moonlight is shining on her just right and it makes her look like she is on stage at a play, like she is the main character. She is the main character in my life and it's going to be hard to change that if she decides to love someone else. I have already decided that I'll wait for her. For as long as she needs, I'll wait and assure she is always happy.

"Dad, is it alright if Jackson and I do a fire?"

I hear Sam say yes and then she is making her way to a seat behind me. I'm lighting the fire and thank her for asking.

"Sorry, I forgot to ask if it was okay."

    She smiles at me, and I wish we could stay like this forever. Just the two of us with the moon and fire emanating how perfect she is. I wish she knew how much she means to me. I get close sometimes to telling her that I like her more than just friends, but then I stop myself. I can't jeopardize this, I don't know what I would do if she wasn't in my life, even if we need to stay friends until the day I die. I take a seat next to her and we sit in silence for a moment.

"Want s'mores?"

    I smile and nod, she makes her way inside to grab the Ingredients and I put my head in my hands.

One More Race

I need to calm myself down before she gets back so we can just enjoy each other's company for the rest of the night, until I have to head out. She gets back with the goods and starts to put the marshmallows on the sticks. She hands me mine when she pulls her out of the fire hers is still flaming. I watch her blow on it to get it to extinguish. When we assemble our s'mores, we clink them together and say cheers. Taylor stops with her smore near her mouth.

"One more race? Let's see who can finish theirs first!"

After we shove the smores in our mouths, we look at each other and laugh. She has some marshmallow on her cheek and I'm guessing I do to since she is pointing to my face.

"You have a little something."

She points to her face to gesture to where the marshmallow is on my face. I point to the complete opposite side of my face.

"Here?" She smiles at my coyness. I touch my nose next.

"How about here?" I start to laugh and then when I look back at her she looks more serious in her expression.

"Here let me." She licks her thumb and wipes the marshmallow from the corner of my mouth that smeared to my cheek. It's the sexiest and sweetest thing that has ever happened to me. I don't know if it's because of the action or just because it's Taylor.

"And you have some here." I lick my thumb and get the smudge that is on the other side of her lips. We both pause with our thumbs on each other's lips, I

One More Race

run mine along her bottom lip and move my eyes from hers down to her lips and back.

"Did you get it?" She sounds out of breath when she says that, and it catches me off guard.

"Jackson, do I look good now?" I move my index finger under her chin and tilt her head up, so we are eye to eye now.

"You look perfect, you always do Tay!"

She starts to smile and blinks slowly and I know now would be a suitable time to tell her how I really feel for her. I open my mouth, but then we are interrupted by the rumble of the race car engine starting in the garage. We both blink and back away from each other. We sit for a while just talking about the cars and the racing expo, honestly anything to make us forget about what just happened between us. I can see that the mosquitoes are starting to come out and they are loving Taylor. The fire is almost out, and I ask if she wants me to put another log on.

"Do you want to go watch a movie with me inside? The bugs are really starting to get me."

I nod before I even say yes to her. We made our way inside and I let her pick the movie. It's an older horror movie of course, those are her favorite and I love her even more for that. *Here we go again with that word love. I don't even know if that is what I'm feeling right now, but if this is love, then I don't ever want it to stop!*

One More Race

Taylor

I wake up in my bed to the smell of bacon and eggs throughout the house. I don't even remember walking to my bedroom last night. The last thing I remember is sitting on the couch with Jack watching The Evil Dead. Maybe I fell asleep, and my parents put me in my room after he left. I make my way down to the kitchen and find my parents at the table setting out breakfast.

"How did you sleep last night?" My dad has a smile on his face from under the part peddler magazine he's looking at when my mother asks that. I scrunch my eyebrows together while grabbing a piece of bacon.

"Good, I must have passed right out after Jackson left." I see my dad take a sip of his coffee to hide his laughter. I want to know what is so funny about me sleeping, but I don't push it because I'm starving, and this breakfast is delicious.

"What are the plans today dad?" I see him shrug and shake his head.

"We got a lot done last night, so I figured we would just take today to relax."

I nod his way agreeing that I'm down for a day of nothing but relaxation. I can draw some more on how I want my kart to look before the races in a few weeks.

One More Race

When I get back to my room, I see that I have two text messages. One is from the group chat, and one is from the private message between Jack and I. Andy never private messages me, he always texts through the group chat we have. It's not a bad thing but you would think that he would want to talk to me in private sometimes like Jack and I do. Andy just sent a picture of his kart with the caption "let's go racing!" Jackson replied to him saying we had a few weeks left before we could take her out. I decided to see the private message from Jackson first before replying in the group chat.

Jackson: Good Morning, how did you sleep sunshine?

Taylor: Surprisingly good, I feel like I passed right out after the movie.

Taylor: what time did you end up leaving last night, I don't remember anything after the movie lol

Jackson: I think it was around 9:45ish. Any plans today?

As soon as he sends that message, I receive another message from the group chat. It's from Andy and he is asking the same question. I decided that replying in the group chat makes the most sense now that they both are asking the same thing.

Taylor: Nope, I was going to draw some more so I had a clear picture of how I want my body to look.

Taylor: As in body I mean my go-kart body lol

Andy: can't wait to see how it turns out!

Jackson: can't wait to see you at the expo tomorrow!

I read Jackson's message and at first, I thought he meant both of us but then I reread it and

One More Race

saw that he only said you, not you guys. I blush at the sight of the message; I do remember some of last night. Especially our moment after s'mores, I felt something when he was that close to me. It scared me a little to feel so strongly towards him because he is my best friend and even though he drops hints sometimes, I don't think he likes me like that. I don't know if I like him like that to be honest, I don't know anything anymore. I have these weird feelings now that come up sometimes that make me want more than a friendship. It happened with Andy when he called me beautiful, and it happens with Jack when he comforts me and sometimes when he just simply looks into my eyes. I get confused when I feel these things especially because they are directed towards both of my friends. You're not supposed to feel like this with your friends, are you?

Alycia Carosella

Jackson

I can't wait to see Taylor later today; it's only been two days and I already miss her. The last time I saw her she was asleep leaning on my shoulder, her hair grazing my cheek. She's a snorer, I bet Andy didn't know that I never want him knowing that. She made it about thirty minutes into the movie before she started to doze off. When she finally fell asleep, I didn't move until the movie was done. I know that's a long time, but it just felt good to have her near me and I didn't want to wake her. Even when it was time to leave, I didn't want to move. I scooped her up and carried her down the hall to her bedroom and placed her on her bed. I covered her and brushed the strands of hair out of her face. I watched her sleep there looking so peaceful, then she would snore, and I would have to try to contain my laughter so I wouldn't startle her.

  She truly is the most beautiful girl I've ever seen in my whole life. The expo show started at eleven, but we don't plan on getting there until one. I told the chat, but it looks like Andy and Taylor will already be there before me. I hate thinking about them spending alone time together and everything he is saying to her. Clearly, he likes her more than friends and that bothers me. It's my own fault though, I'm the one who is too much of a pansy to admit that I like her. I mean my own dad called me out for crying aloud.

We finally get to the expo, and I immediately ditch my dad to go find Tay. I see Sam as I'm walking toward the tent that they said they were at.

"Hey Jackson, they are down that way. Where's your dad at?" I point behind me, and he nods and smiles at me. That is one thing I'm grateful for, if in the future I do grow some balls and tell Taylor how I feel, at least I know her dad likes me. It will hopefully be an easier transition from friend to boyfriend. *Why am I even thinking it will eventually be, boyfriend? I can't tell the future and I don't know if she even feels the same.*

I spot her blonde hair first and then I see the chestnut brown hair next to her. I know it's them from the back of them. When I reach them, I can see the embarrassment on Taylor's face by whatever Andy was just talking about with the guy at the stand.

"Hey what's up guys?" They both turn to acknowledge I'm here, but Andy replies first.

"I was just telling Steve how good of a drawer Taylor was and how she should use it to paint car bodies." He said enthusiastic about the whole conversation, but I can tell Tay is uncomfortable with the idea.

"I don't think she would have much time to do that. Especially being a race car driver. That takes up most of your time man. You know that!"

I turn to Taylor and see that her expression has gone from embarrassment to appreciation, and I love that I was the one to do that. Andy completely ignores my remark and just moves us along through the booths. Taylor is in between us both and our hands have grazed each other countless times. Each time she looks at me and smiles acknowledging it happening but not doing anything about it. *I wonder if she is waiting for me to make a move first.* Before I can think any longer, I grab her hand and intertwine our fingers together. She turns and looks up at me with her rainbow eyes and smiles at me. It's not like we haven't held each other's hands before. We used to do it all the time as kids, but this time though, it feels different!

    I can't help but feel like this is exactly how it's supposed to be, her hand in mine, me being the one to make her smile, us against everyone else. I need to tell her how I feel before someone else does because she is wonderful. There is no way anybody

One More Race

else doesn't see how incredible this girl is. Someone is going to take her before I even get the chance to tell her how I feel!

Alycia Carosella

Taylor

How do you breathe? I forgot at that moment. My heart was beating out of my chest, but I don't know how with no oxygen getting to my body. When I looked at him and smiled, I swear it was just the two of us in this room full of people. I saw nervousness in those ocean eyes when I looked at him and that was partially why I smiled, to hopefully show him that I was okay with holding his hand. I don't know why suddenly, holding hands is such a big deal for us. We used to do it all time when we were younger. We even would tell people that we were married when they would look our way. I laugh internally at that memory; we really are two halves to a whole. I was waiting this whole time for him to grab it, we brushed against each other a few times, but I wasn't going to make the first move.

"Taylor, can you come over here for a moment." I turn to see my dad and Jack instantly let's go of my hand. *Ouch! Okay.*

I look at him and he looks nervous again. I nudge him toward my dad and tell Andy we will catch up with him later. He doesn't seem phased at all because he is already in a full-blown conversation with another guy at a different booth.

"What's up dad?" He gestures around the booth we are at and smiles, that's when I see Chris behind him too.

"You guys both need fire suits and new helmets." I look at Chris and then look at my dad, he nods at me and smiles.

"Look around and let us know what you guys want."

I turn to Jack and grab his hand again and yank him around pointing at a bunch from black to red to the whole damn rainbow. We don't normally get brand new things; I mean occasionally we do but this stuff is expensive!

"This one is perfect for you!" He turns and sees the pink one I'm pointing at. He smirks at me and shakes his head. I turn to look at some more and he goes down a different aisle.

One More Race

"Taylor, come here. I found one!" I'm heading his way thinking he found one for himself but when he turns around, he is holding a purple suit. I smile because it is perfect and because it's my favorite color.

"I love it, I need to try it on to see if it fits." I start to take my shoes off and take the suit from his hands.

"Wait, right here?"

"Yeah, it just goes over my clothes so it's fine. Don't move though or I'll fall." I grab a hold of his shoulder to hold myself still and I slip it on and zip it up. I did a little twirl with it on and turned to Jackson.

"What do you think? Does it look good?" He is standing there just staring at me with a big grin on his face.

"It looks great, anything on you would look great!"

Alycia Carosella

He keeps saying things like this and making me question the tone of it. It's confusing as hell; he held my hand earlier so maybe that was his way of showing me that he was interested. It was just holding hands, maybe he didn't feel that jolt of electricity this time like I did. This time everything, we do together feels different, it has been slowly starting to feel different, but I've been brushing it off as friendly interactions. I don't know, Andy acts the same way sometimes so maybe it's just a boy thing. I respect our friendship too much to ruin it though. I will never make the first move, so if he really does want more than he is going to have to be the one to say it! I try to brush off his comment to make this less awkward.

"Okay so it's settled, this one is mine. Now let's find one for you, but I doubt it will look this good!"

One More Race

I laugh and wink at him and start to walk down the aisle with the men's suits.

I look for a blue suit since that's his favorite color. When I found one, I held it up to him and told him to put it on. He is pulling it on, and it makes his t-shirt ride up his torso just above his navel. I can't help but stare at him in all his glory, I've only ever seen him without a shirt once, but we were younger, and I didn't look at him the same way I do now. He has grown into his body so much more than that time and he has more muscles too. I can see the sculpture of his V as I call it and his happy trail, both leading to that sweet spot below his jeans. I wonder what he looks like under there. *Whoa what? Stop thinking about his penis! Stop right now before he notices what you're thinking about.* Just as I block the image of his penis out of my head it's as if he can read my mind. He smiles at me when he realizes I'm staring at his exposed skin.

"Okay so how is it? Give it to me straight!" I chuckle and twirl my finger to tell him I needed him to give me a little twirl like I did for him.

"Hmm I don't know Jack, looks a bit tight in your buttocks region." I burst out laughing because who uses phrasing like that.

"So, you're admitting to staring at my butt?" I can see the amusement in his eyes at that remark, but I won't let him have that win.

"Ehh, it's just your ordinary every person kind of butt." I shrug trying to hide my smirk

"Well, we all can't be you now can we." Okay so that was unexpected. He just admitted to staring at my ass…Goodness I don't know if this is flirting or friendly banter.

One More Race

"We need to get helmets so lead the way, mister." He looks at me nervously and walks over to the helmets. I grab one and try it once and to my surprise it fits perfectly. As I'm taking it off, I shake my hair out. Next thing I know Jackson's hands are on my face and his lips are on mine, but only for a second.

He just kissed me, the first kiss I've ever had with someone, and it was Jackson. I'm not complaining, but I thought it would have felt different. He opens his eyes finally and he looks shocked that he just did that.

"I wanted to do that the night of the fire, but we got interrupted." Okay so maybe he is feeling this too. I don't know what to say to him. I want to tell him to do it again, but I also don't want to scare him away, so I just smile.

Alycia Carosella

Jackson

Holy shit, holy shit! I just kissed Taylor and she is just smiling and not saying anything. I don't know if I should apologize or act like it never happened. "We need to find your helmet now" she grabs my hand and pulls me towards a black helmet and lowers it on my head. I guess we are just going to ignore that it happened then. I should tell her now before it's too late. I started something between us with the kiss and I don't want her to think it was just a kiss with no meaning behind it.

"Tay, I need to tell you something!" She grabs the helmet and lifts it off my head and looks me right into my eyes. My confidence weakens a bit but maybe if I just hurry up and say it then I'll feel better with having everything out on the table. I must have been lost in my thoughts for too long because she nudged me.

"What is it? What do you need to tell me Jack?" Her expression softens and it makes me feel better. Here goes nothing.

"The reason I kissed you was..." before I can finish my sentence, Andy is back with us. I swear this kid has the worst timing. I can see the disappointment in her eyes that I didn't finish my sentence. Maybe I should just take the hint that the universe is trying to stop me from telling Taylor that I love her. *Dammit I meant to say, care for her, I don't know if it's love yet. I hope it is because it feels fantastic when we are together.*

"Did you guys find anything good?" Andy glances at our hands full and nods like he approves our picks.

"Yeah! we have all our gear now, so we will be able to focus on getting the karts ready now."

"Well, if you need any help, I'm here. My kart has been done so I'm free whenever you are."

Sometimes I feel bad that I get angry with Andy because he really is a nice person. That's why we have him in our little friend group. We all head to Sam and my dad and hand them our things and let them know that we are going to grab something to eat.

"Alright, we will meet you guys at the food area in an hour."

I'm guessing that's when Sam and Taylor plan to leave. I'm hoping to get some alone time with Taylor again so I can finish my sentence, but that doesn't look too promising. I wish she was in the middle of us again, but she is next to Andy this time and I'm at the other end. They are talking away and I remain quiet, I know I'm making this awkward and if I don't start acting normal that he will know we did something. I don't know why I'm nervous he will find out; I just don't want this to affect our friendship in any way. Gosh I'm so dumb, I shouldn't have done that, I just jeopardized my closest relationship with the person that means the most to me. From now on I'm on friend duty, no more slip ups and no more thoughts of being more than just friends. If there is more here, then she will tell me and that's when I will confess to her how I feel.

I've been the one making moves every time so far and it's making me nervous that she hasn't made any in return. Maybe she feels pressured because I held her hand and then I went and kissed her. I hope she doesn't, that would make me feel even more of a horrible friend, I don't want her to feel obligated in any way to reciprocate my actions. *Well unless she actually, genuinely wants to.* We reach the table with our food, and we all grab our seats and face each other. That's one good thing about round tables, you technically aren't sitting right next to someone. I try to forget earlier and just act normal while we all eat and talk about the race coming up. Taylor talks like she isn't fazed at all

Alycia Carosella

with what happened, and I can't tell if it's genuine or if she is just good at acting.

The next hour went by fast and then we were all heading out. Well except for Andy because his dad is a race official, so he usually stays at the expos for a while. Sometimes I feel for him, but he seems to enjoy all the extra perks he gets from his dad working for the speedway. Once we get to the parking lot, we all say our goodbyes and that's it. No hug, no kiss, just a wave and a little smile, but hell I'll take it!

One More Race

Jackson

Today is race day! These past few weeks have gone by in a flash, and I can't wait to race for the first time, but more importantly I can't wait to see Taylor. Things seem to be back to normal after my slip up at the expo. We haven't really had alone time to discuss what happened and why it happened. I'm grateful for that because it's hard to stay in the friend mind zone when it's just me and Taylor. We've all been hyper focused on getting the cars ready for today, we've been at the garage basically every day.

I'm usually excited to go to Taylor's but I've been nervous after our kiss. I didn't think our first kiss would have happened like that. I want it to be memorable and for her to realize in that moment that we were meant for each other, but I don't think either one of us felt anything. A small little peck on the lips wasn't long enough to feel anything anyways, right? God I'm going crazy thinking about everything I want to give Taylor and knowing I can't.

    I go outside to load everything up for tonight and to make sure all my things are on the trailer. It's so exciting to know that I'm racing now and not just waiting for my dad to race. I always wanted to follow in my father's footsteps and get on the track and be the best father to my kid just like he is with me. I still don't understand why mom left him, maybe he was a bad husband? I don't know, I was younger when she left, but she acted like she wanted to start fresh, so she left me too. I would be lying if I said it didn't hurt, she did get what she wanted though. She remarried and made a new family with her new husband. I have a stepbrother now, but we have nothing in common.

    My father doesn't talk much about her anymore, but I know he loved her. Hell, maybe he still does. He hasn't tried to find someone else after her. They wouldn't have made me unless they loved each other! I tried to chalk it up to just falling out of love, but I can't help but think that it was me that made that happen. Maybe I created strain on them and that made them realize they had made a mistake having me. Every time I think that though my mind doesn't let it stick because my father Is the best father I've met, besides Sam Martin! If I turn out to be half the father, they are when I'm older I would be grateful.

I know I shouldn't be thinking about having kids anytime soon, but all I've ever known was racing and family. I know what I want and I'm willing to do everything in my power to make it happen. Maybe if I make a beautiful life my mother will recognize that I wasn't a mistake! She's the reason I second guess my every move. If she just tried to at least to see me or acknowledge my progress even a little, I think my guilt would subside a fraction. I'll never make my child think that they are anything but loved. Screw my mother for making me think any less of myself. My dad has

One More Race

always been there bringing me up and raising me on his own. Hopefully in my future I'll have a beautiful wife by my side to help raise our kids.

I've been thinking about my future a lot since starting high school, it's such an important time in your life. It's the start of your freedom and the time you use to set up your future career. I have goals and a timeline and I'm going to stick to it the best I can to make my father proud and show him how great he was with raising me. It's the least I can do.

I get snapped out of my head with the honk of my dad's horn to let me know it's time to get going to the track. I step in his truck, and I'm filled with excitement, I'm on my way to my very first race! "I told mom about the race tonight. She said she would try to make it!" My dad's hands tense around the steering wheel and his eyes turn to me.

Alycia Carosella

"That's great Jackson, but don't get your hopes up, okay?" I wish he believed that she would show up, but I understand his logic. He is trying to prepare me for the pit that is going to be inside of me later when I realize she didn't show up yet again.

"Yeah, I know the drill, just thought I would let you know just in case."

I try not to show my hopefulness that she sticks to her word for once and shows up. I can see my dad's expression change to sadness. I don't know if he is sad because I brought up my mother or because he hates seeing me pulling for her. It must hurt him to think that she dropped us both to go start a new family with someone else. She doesn't live that far from us, so I don't understand why showing up for me is so out of her way. I've tried to get him back out there, but he insists that he is happy with his life just the way it is. Maybe in the future he will find someone who loves him as fiercely as he loves me, I couldn't have asked for a better father!

Sometimes I wish my dad had found someone better than my mother because he deserves to be happy too, but then I realize that if that happened then I wouldn't be here. I would have never met Taylor and I would have never known what it felt like to kiss someone and to get lost inside someone's eyes. *To love someone!*

Alycia Carosella

Taylor

This day has been dragging on and now it's finally race time. There were so many people here at the track for opening night. Andy was already here when we pulled in and started unloading everything. I still haven't started on my body yet so for the last few weeks Jackson and I have been patching the existing one that came with my kart. We both put our numbers on our karts and then laughed when we realized that they were the same ones we had used since we were kids. Mine is number two, but Jackson doesn't know that I always choose that number because it meant something to me. He always would tell me that it was the two of us forever when I was having a difficult day and that always stuck with me. So, the number two for just the two of us.

It was weird to be working in the garage after the expo and acting like we were just friends and that he hadn't kissed me or held my hand for half the time. I wish he would have finished his sentence before Andy walked back to us! He should have texted me what he wanted to say, but I guess if it was that important to him then he would have wanted to tell me in person.

We haven't had much alone time lately with the races zeroing in and us needing to get the cars ready. Our dad's first race is next weekend and they have been going crazy trying to get their cars ready on top of helping us when we needed it. Jackson knows a lot about cars, so it was nice to have him around when I was first learning things. If my dad hadn't taught me something yet, Jackson was there to show me. He's helped me so much with my confidence, working on cars when you're a girl doesn't get the best results. People think you are just saying those things for attention, but when I can show that I know what I'm talking about, most of the time they shut up. I don't get the ultimatum with girls being in the garage, but by the time I get done with high school I'll know all the ins and outs of a car.

    I've been thinking about my future a lot now that I'll be in high school. I feel that these four years are what shape you for the freedom that comes after graduation. I already know my future down to every detail. I know my mother wants me to go off the college, but it never appealed to me if I'm being honest. I love cars and it feels so natural when my hands are on them working. I will eventually open my own garage and get married of course. Some little rugrats wouldn't bother me either. My parents are the epitome of happily ever after and hopefully I have that someday. I know I have time before I can get all these accomplished, but I will continue to put in the work until I have every single one.

    I feel a hand on my shoulder, and I turn around to Andy's big smile.

"Hey you! Are you excited for your first race?" I smile so damn big it hurts my cheeks.

"Of course, I am! I barely got any sleep last night."

"Is Jackson here too? I haven't seen him yet. I figured we could scope out our competition." Andy laughed at his remark and tilted his head towards the track.

"He should be here soon, let's go check out the track. Get a feel for it!"

He smiles and leads the way. I follow him on to the track and we take a few laps getting a feel for the clay and making sure there aren't any ruts we should be concerned about. I haven't raced on this track yet, but I have watched so I know the basics of how to maneuver effectively when that green flag comes out. The track isn't anything huge but it's plenty for our little karts! I spot Chris's truck and then see Jackson's face in the passenger seat. I can't help but feel excited to finally see him here.

One More Race

This is his first race too and I can't wait to pick his brain on his racing strategies. I motion toward the pits and tell Andy that Jackson is here. We both make our way to the pits to find him unloading the trailer. They parked right next to us and the sight of that made me more anxious than excited at that moment. We still haven't addressed that kiss and I'm nervous that if I bring it up that he will close off. I don't want to come off as this clingy girl that wants more from him than friendship.

Except that is exactly what I want!

But I can't just come out and say that to him, it would make us awkward! Obviously, he was just caught in the moment when he kissed me or else, he would have done it again or told me he wanted more. I close off those thoughts as soon as he makes his way towards me and Andy.

Alycia Carosella

"Hey guys!"

"We already took a few laps on the track to make sure it felt good, but Andy wanted to scoop out the competition. You in?"

"Hell yes!" I laugh at his enthusiastic reply.

"Lucky number four and two I see. I was wondering what numbers you were going to choose."

I see Jackson smile and then glance at me when Andy realizes our racing numbers for the first time. There are only a few more teens in our class so I don't think there is much competition to be seen. We make our way around the pits looking at everyone's karts and continually losing Andy. He knows everyone at the track since his dad works here. I guess it's good that he is in our friend group so he can give us the inside scoop of what's going on. Of course, that's not the only reason we brought him into our friend group. Every time we went to watch our dad's race, he was in the stands watching the race too. Over time we would continue to talk, and he slowly integrated into Jackson and I friendship.

    I haven't suggested adding anyone else because I feel that we are perfect the way we are. Of course, if they suggested someone, I would just dismiss them just because I say we are good. I have the sudden urge to reach for Jackson's hand and hold it, but I hold back. I don't want to make this situation awkward, especially since we will be spending all night together. When we finish doing our walk through, Andy heads back to his trailer to get ready for the race. Jackson and I head back as well to make sure our fathers don't need any help with anything.

"Do you guys want anything to eat before the race?" Chris is looking at both of us when he asks. "You guys don't go out for another three classes, so we figured we would get some grub." My dad continues to stand near Chris waiting for us to answer then.

"Nah I'm good."

"Can I have a soda please!" I smile and turn towards the truck once our fathers turn away to go to concession.

"Where are you going Tay?" I smile towards Jackson and point to the truck. I need music therapy before I go out on the track. Even though I have dreamed about this day for basically forever, I'm still nervous as hell.

"I just need to relax a little before it's our time to go out." I see concern in Jack's eyes after I say that.

One More Race

Then he is following me into the truck. My dad owns an older truck with the full bench seat in the front, so I slide right in to turn on the radio. Jackson is seated right next to me in the passenger side of the truck. Even though it's an older truck my father switched out the head unit so we could have Bluetooth and something up to date in it.

    I hook up my phone and let my Spotify do its magic of relaxing me with my playlist. I have a wide variety of music on my playlist, it could be country one minute, then classic rock, then screamo or pop. I have songs for all my moods, but right now at this moment any music will do. I can feel Jackson's gaze on me while I lay my head back and close my eyes to just listen to the music. I wish he would take this opportunity to talk to me, to really talk to me about that kiss.

Alycia Carosella

As the last song ends, your love by the outfield comes on and I can feel the corners of my mouth tug up into a smile. I can't help but sing the intro to this song no matter what mood I'm in. It's too catchy not to, I start to sing it and Jackson starts smiling at me while watching me embarrass myself. Halfway through the song we both are singing the song but in my head all I can register is the line "I don't want to lose your love tonight." We both sang it at the same time, and I know we were just goofing around but I wish he was telling me that for real. "What song would you play if someone asked you about me?" He gives me a confused look and grabs my phone. I grow nervous while he is searching through my music. Then he clicks on one and I can't help but roll my eyes at him. He smirks when born to be wild starts to play by Steppenwolf.

One More Race

"I was born to be wild? interesting choice Mr. Ford!" He starts to laugh but then the chorus starts to play, and we both are singing to it at the top of our lungs.

"What about me?" I'm confused at first by his remark, but then register that he is referring to the songs.

"That's a tough one, hmm let's see!"

I grab my phone and start to scroll through my lengthy list of songs. There are so many that explain him but picking just one right now is tough. I know I'm taking a huge leap here but if he isn't going to make the first move, I guess I'll have to break my rule and do it myself. I click on the song and then turn towards Jackson to see his reaction.

Jackson

I couldn't help but feel my chest start to fill as soon as the beat started for the song. Taylor loves all kinds of music, so it doesn't surprise me that we went from classic rock to country. I was expecting her to pick a funny song like I did, but the lyrics in this song speak to so much more. Would you go with me by Josh Turner started to play and I couldn't help but look at her when he started to sing. She looked nervous as soon as she clicked on the song. Was she waiting for me to acknowledge the kiss this whole time? She was the one that acted like it didn't happen afterwards. Was I imagining that or was she genuinely interested in me? When the chorus started, I grabbed for her hand and held it in mine for the rest of the song. I was rubbing my thumb on the top of her hand while we listened to the song, not breaking eye contact at all.

If she only knew how much this song speaks the truth for us. She doesn't know this, but I always picked the number four for our cars because of her. Every time I could tell she was upset I always reminded her that it was the two of us forever and it always got that smile out of her. I choose four because it is going to be forever with us rather it's as friends of more!

Alycia Carosella

As soon as the song ended all I could muster up to say was "Yes!" She blinked and I could tell that she was happy and slightly confused by my outburst. "I would go with you anywhere Taylor Nicole Martin!" That's when I noticed a single tear still down her cheek. I start to panic because I don't know what I did wrong to make her cry. *I'm supposed to make her happy, God damnit, I made her cry!*

"Whoa, hey, what's wrong? Don't cry! Please."

Before I could wipe her tears away, she jumped to me and wrapped her arms around me. She was squeezing so hard, like her life depended on it. Her head tucked right in the crevice of my neck, I could smell her coconut hair conditioner and planted a kiss on top of her bright blond hair. She nuzzled her head even more into my body and I swear I melted right there. What is this we are doing? This feels so right, and I can't help but think that this is exactly where she belongs. I'm my arms, head on my chest, hair in my face! I want to tilt her head up and kiss her again so badly, but we are interrupted by the sound of our dads walking toward the truck. She straightens up first and wipes her tears away.

"Sorry, I'm just an emotional mess lately…. Hormones!"

She shrugs her shoulders like it's no big deal. *Hormones? Really Taylor?* Is she trying to backpedal or am I imagining this too? We got out of the truck, and it was like a curtain went up again because the friend zone was back in full force. These mixed signals are going to kill us if one of us doesn't just come out and confess our love. *Damn it I mean feelings, not just love!*

Alycia Carosella

Our dads look both of us up and down as we are making our way back to the karts from the truck. I see my dad smiling and Sam looked a bit concerned. That look made me extremely nervous.

Sam is like a second father to me and even though he likes me, that doesn't mean he likes the idea of me being involved with his daughter. I need to shut this down before it gets worse. I don't want to hurt her, and I know that I would do everything in my power not to, but I am half my mother. What if I do something wrong and I do hurt Taylor? I wouldn't be able to live with myself if I lost her and Sam for that matter! Friends, that's all we are, and I need to get that through my thick skull right fucking now. No more damn slip ups!

It's finally our time to go onto the track, so we are all getting geared up. Taylor is in her new

One More Race

fire suit and helmet and God damn it is sexy as hell. My mind isn't the only part of me that thinks that. *Not now! I can't go out on the track with a hard on for my FRIEND! Just friends Jackson!* I watch as Taylor and Andy get into their Karts and then as soon as I get in, we are all having our engines started and heading out on the track. We managed to get halfway through the race before we got a caution flag for someone spinning out. I try to assess the situation to see who it was and when we turn the corner, I see it's Taylor's kart. I know she is fine but I still throughout a thumbs up towards her and she returns it to let me know she's well.

Andy has been dominating the track tonight and I've been getting stuck in the middle. I'm not sure where Taylor has been, but I haven't run into her at all trying to pass me. We start up again and

Alycia Carosella

that's when I gun for it, trying to get as close to Andy as I can. I want to win this first race so I can celebrate with Taylor after! We have three laps to go and I'm still in four place and have been stuck here for some time. The white flag is out, and I take to the outside to try to gain a spot. To my surprise I get it and I finished the race in third place. Andy ended up winning the race and I was so happy for him. I was expecting a little jealousy on my part, but I was still on my high from being able to be the one behind the wheel. We all pull off the track and back to our pit spots.

One More Race

Taylor

Holy shit! My adrenaline is still pumping even after getting out of my kart. I finished dead last, and I still couldn't hide my smile. I had so much fun being out on the track, I would have cared where I finished. I saw that Andy won the race, so I started to head in that direction. Jackson followed behind me towards Andy's crowded pit area. I spot him at his kart thanking everyone for the congratulations and then I spot Bethany Hamilton. She hates me with a passion for some reason, I think she just hates everyone to be honest. She's so damn competitive, she's been racing for a little over a year now and she and Andy have been getting closer since they have been racing together. Her father also works for the speedway so they must spend a lot of time here just like Andy.

    I don't know why she is so rude to me when I haven't done anything to her. Maybe she is just mad because she came in second to Andy? As soon as Jackson and I make it through some of the crowd, Andy spots us. He smiles and walks toward me giving me the biggest hug and smile. I'm taken back a bit by all the affection I'm getting today but these boys. I return the hug and tell him congratulations on the win.

One More Race

"You kicked ass man!" I turn towards Jackson, I forgot he was standing right next to me for a moment.

"Thanks man, I was waiting for you to give me a run for my money." I was a bit shocked by his straightforward remark with Jack.

"Yeah, I got stuck in four for most of the race but finished third overall." They both turn towards me and ask at the same time where I finished. I put a huge smile on my face when I answered them.

"Dead last!" I could see their confusion at my cheerful outlook to finishing last.

"I went out to have fun and I did exactly that!" They both replaced their expressions with smiles, and I was grateful for them at that moment. They were letting me bask in my glory of being the loser.

"Wow dead last!" Bethany had a smirk on her face after saying that and all I wanted to do was smack her smirk right off her face. Andy turned toward her and gave her a disappointed look. I could see her expression change in that moment to sadness or maybe anger.

"Seriously Bethany? Leave her alone!" I was grateful that even though he was friends with us both that he would still stick up for me. She rolled her eyes and went over to him to talk to him.

"I just wanted to come over and say congrats on the win, I can't help it that I overheard the conversation."

She went in to hug Andy and he reciprocated the hug, but I could tell that he was still a bit uncomfortable that she hasn't apologized. He ended the hug, but she still stood by him though. I felt a bit uncomfortable staying around when she clearly wasn't going to leave.

"I'm going to go get my things packed up so I can watch the last few races. I'll text you later. Congrats again Andy, you did amazing!"

I could see his eyes light up at my remark. He came in for a hug and then there it was again, a kiss on the cheek. I felt the uneasiness of Jackson's presence and the hatred of Bethany in that moment. I froze for a moment when his lips retracted, and he stared into my eyes. I panicked and finally pointed behind my shoulder gesturing toward my trailer and giving Andy a smile. When I turned to start heading back to the trailer, I saw that Jackson had started back before me. If I wasn't mistaken, I sensed that he was pissed off. He got like that whenever I gave Andy more attention than him.

Alycia Carosella

I don't understand the whole alpha male shit that guys do when they are around women. It's kind of a turn off for me if I'm being honest, I know some girls love that quality in a guy, but not me. I want them to win me over with romantic gestures, not a dick swinging contest. Maybe I'm the problem, maybe I'm giving them mixed signals. I love them both as friends, but I wouldn't mind more with them as well. Of course, not at the same time, I just mean that if one of them asked me to be their girlfriend I wouldn't say no! These feelings are starting to confuse me, and I don't like feeling that way. I have my whole future planned out, there's no room for confusion there.

    Maybe my mom is right, and I need to do more girl things to attract some girlfriends for a change. Just the thought makes me want to gag, but

One More Race

I haven't really tried to find new friends lately. With high school starting I should start fresh and try to make new friends. Ones that I can talk to about these feelings to see if they are normal or how to get them under control. Maybe change is what I need. Jackson and Andy get the summertime and my new friends will get me during the school year. It will give me time to recenter myself and assure that I'm not leading either one of them on.

Now to get through the summer with that mindset!

Alycia Carosella

Jackson

He obviously likes her more than friends, but I don't need to stand around to watch it. I was grateful to Andy for sticking up for Taylor when Beth decided to be snarky with her. He got to snap back before I even had the chance to. Maybe that is who she needs to be with. Andy is a great guy and as much as it hurts me to see her with him, maybe I should let it happen. I can't lose two important people in my life just because I'm being selfish and want Taylor to myself. I wouldn't want to betray Sam by potential hurting his daughter!

One More Race

When I finally get back to the trailer, I start to pack up my kart, so it's done when it's time to leave. Our dads must be watching the races because they aren't here. As I'm packing up, Taylor appears behind me with her arms crossed just staring at me. "Yes? "Wow, did I just say that to her like that? Gosh I'm such an asshole, maybe this is good. If I'm an ass, then she will distance herself from me and then we can nip this before it goes even farther. "Excuse me!" Great, I've pissed her off, mission accomplished! I don't reply to her because I'm not doing this right now.
"Why are you in such a piss poor mood? You finished third, that's awesome Jack!" I can see that she is trying to soften me into talking but honestly all I want right now is for her to go away. She weakens me and makes me want to tell her

everything, all the time. How my day was and how I feel and what I want. I hate that she can do that to me just by being near me, it makes me love her more and I can't! *God, I do love her. I can't! It's going to end bad.*

"Thanks, I need to pack up." I'm trying to let her get the hint gently, but I don't think it's going to work. Taylor is so damn headstrong and when she wants something, she does everything in her power to get it.

"What did I do?" I don't think I just blurt out the first thing that comes to my mind.

"God damnit Taylor, I don't know what you want!" She flinches at me raising my voice to her and it tears at my heart the way she is staring at me right now.

"I-I don't understand what you mean?"

"Exactly, you don't understand. You want me one minute and the next you don't. I can't keep up on whether we should be pretending we are friends or doing more!" She swallows hard and I can see her eyes glossing over and I'm feeling like shit right now! I don't think she understands how bad this is hurting me.

"I-I umm.... Jack.... I'm sorry!"

"What do you want Taylor?" She furrows her brows, and I can tell by the quiver of her bottom lip that she is about to cry. I close my eyes to try to get recentered for what I'm about to tell her because it's far from what I want to tell her right now.

"Andy is obviously smitten over you. He wants more with you, if you feel even the slightest back towards him then you should tell him."

I turn away from her because I don't want to see her face after saying that. I get the last of the things packed and then I sit in the truck for the last two races. When my dad returns, he gets in and thanks me for packing up.

"No problem." I continue to look out the window with my Air Pods in while listening to music.

"Want to wait for Taylor to say goodbye? I think she was heading back from Andy's trailer." That remark made me winch thinking I sent her straight into another man's arms. *It's for the better. You are saving her!*

"No, that's okay, I'll text them when we get home."

"Alrighty then."

I turn to my dad when he finally starts the truck, and I can tell he is confused by my dismissal of Taylor. I always want to spend as much time with her as possible, so saying no is obvious, for something is going on. Thankfully, he doesn't push it and we stay quiet while pulling out. As I put my other air pod in and scroll through my songs, I put on Josh turner, would you go with me and as soon as it starts to play, I feel wetness building in the back of my eyes. This song is exactly what I would say to Taylor while asking her to be mine. I close my eyes and let that one tear fall, as I open my eyes and wipe the tear away, I look in the side mirror and see Andy walking Taylor back to her trailer and I let out a heavy sigh.

    I lay my head back and close my eyes and just listen to the song. As it ends, I just want to click on it again and listen to it on repeat until I undo what I did tonight. But it's too late, I already told her to pursue Andy and from what I saw, that happened damn quickly. I can feel my dad looking at the back of my head, so I turn to meet his gaze.

"So, what happened? Clearly you and Taylor had a fight." I sigh and pull my Air Pods out and try to think of where to start.

"I don't know if I want to talk about it, we are just friends. It will pass eventually."

"Will it? You guys have been friends since you were babies and not once have, I seen you guys' fight. Except for when you broke her dress up heels because she insisted you had to wear them, even though you told her your feet were too big."

    I smile when that memory comes back into my head. We really were inseparable back then. Taylor is an only child, so we were always together playing, but she always got to choose. I swear I was every single princess you could dream up at some point. When we would get older, we would pretend that we're getting married, but she would argue with me because she wanted to wear the tux and I told her she couldn't because there was only one and the husband was supposed to. You can guess how that ended out, I didn't look too bad in a white dress, but damn it was uncomfortable.

 I almost forgot about the pact we had made when we were nine. We promised that if we weren't married by twenty-five that we would marry each other. I laugh when I remember that and my dad smiles at me.

"We really do have a lot of history together!" I look down at my feet with guilt thinking about the way I left things. I won't see her until next weekend unless we go over to her house to work on the cars.

Alycia Carosella

I can't fix this over text messages, that's if I even should fix it.

"So, what was this fight over? Was she upset that she lost?" I think of how overjoyed she was after the race and that big ass smile, she had on her face.

"No, she was just happy that she got to get out on the track."

"Okay, then what was it? Did you do something wrong?" I feel my stomach flip when he says that.

"Do you think that's why mom left?" I wasn't even thinking when that outburst came out of my mouth. My father turns his head slowly and burrows his brows together. I try not to talk about mom that much because I don't want to make my dad feel like bad, but I still don't know why she left us.

"Your mother left because she didn't have everything she needed."

"What does that even mean? So, she left because of me then!"

He slams the brakes and pulls over to the side of the road. I can see his shoulder drop and a loud sigh come out of his mouth.

"Listen to me Jackson, whatever you and Taylor are going through. It has nothing to do with your mother and me. You both are completely different than we were." I go to open my mouth to reply to him, but he cut me off.

"I loved your mother so much Jackson, I still love her to a certain regard, but I didn't love her enough."

"What do you mean?' My father's face shows guilt and regret.

"I love racing and your mother understood that she supported me in that also while being a wife and then eventually a mother. We both wanted to get married and make a family. She never left because she didn't want you! We planned for you Jackson, she just wanted more, and I wasn't supportive enough to help her achieve what she wanted."

"I didn't do my part as a husband; you never did anything wrong Jackson. I don't know why your mother hasn't put forth the initiative to stay in your life, but don't you ever think it was because of you!"

I didn't realize that I was crying again when he told me that I was planned and that they wanted me. I always thought that they had gotten pregnant on accident and that my mother didn't want to be a mother. It makes sense that she wouldn't want to go see me race now, that is something that took my father away from her. Racing is a way of living for most drivers, you have your family but there is an

One More Race

immense amount of support that is needed when its race time. All that time spent working on the cars, the amount of money, the stress when your loved one is out on the track! It takes a lot from someone to be able to be that supportive person.

I may understand why my mother left, but I don't forgive her for abandoning me and starting over like I never existed. If I'm being honest with myself, I don't have the energy to keep trying with her anymore. I have a woman in my life that I want to give all my attention and support to. Knowing what I know now, I'll be damned if I let her slip through my fingers! *But what about Sam?*

"I kissed Taylor!" I see a sigh of relief from my father after that outburst.

"You guys are fighting over a kiss?"

"I don't know, I guess so. She confuses me, I don't know if she wants to be just friends or more." I flash back to the last thing I told Taylor before leaving the races tonight and I feel extremely guilty for yelling at her.

"It will happen often; you have a lot of memories together Jackson! Friends or not, the lines can get blurred, but you can't blame just her. You both need to be straightforward with each other on how you feel."

"I think it's too late for that. I told her to go with Andy because he obviously liked her."

I run both my hands down my face and sigh. I'm so God damn stupid for fighting with my best friend over something so dumb.

One More Race

"Jackson, you need to understand that you both are still young as well. You have your whole life ahead of you!"

"I know dad. I'll fix this. She is my best friend!" I see his smile out of the corner of my eye.

"I'm so proud of you son, don't you ever forget that!" I reach for my dad and give him a huge hug before we pull back on the road and head to Sam's to drop off the cars and then home for the night. *I will fix this, I promise Taylor!*

Taylor

This past week has been awkward as hell. I only messaged back in the group chat when one of the boys messaged. I never started a conversation with them because I was afraid that I would somehow be leading them on. Maybe I can't be friends with more than one guy or just guys in general. It just doesn't make sense to me though; Jackson and I have been friends since forever and now all of a sudden, we are having problems. What changed?

One More Race

He still hasn't apologized for yelling at me at the races last weekend, but maybe he was saving it for tonight so he could do it face to face. I don't even know if I deserve an apology, he technically didn't do anything wrong. He's not wrong for telling me how he feels, I just need to tell him how I feel. I wish I knew exactly how I felt with him right now. I love him in my life so much that I'm willing to do anything to ensure that he stays in my life forever. If that means sacrificing being with him and only being friends then so be it, I'll do it. I can't lose him!

Andy had helped me calm down after I had started crying at the track last week and I was taken back at how sweet he was. I was expecting him to take advantage that Jackson and I had gotten into an argument and try to make a move. Instead, he had consoled me like a friend was supposed to and just been there to talk to. Sometimes I feel like he does everything to please me and it's the sweetest thing ever. Here I go again with these mixed feelings with these boys.

I have no one to talk to about them either, I can't go to my parents because they will freak out that I'm interested in dating, I don't have any cousins that I talk to on a regular basis, and I sure as hell don't have any friends that aren't these boys. I can't believe I'm going to say this, but I can't wait to start high school and finally make new friends. Tonight, is my dad's and Chris's first race of the season and I'm super excited to go. My dad told me that we will all be in the pits tonight and I could tell that my mother was relieved. I asked my dad once if

One More Race

he ever was bothered that she didn't go to every race and to my surprise he said no.

He had told me that she supported his racing dreams from the time they had first gotten together throughout their entire relationship. He told me that she would always make sure that everything was packed and set for him the night before and that I was always taken care of, so he didn't have to worry about anything. If she didn't want to go watch him race in person, then that was her choice. Then I remember him winking at me and telling me that he knew she still watched at home anyways on her phone.

I always kept that with me even to this day. I know a lot of people say that you will end up with someone like your father, and most people say they want the opposite. For me I hope that happens, I want a relationship like my parents! They have been together since high school and support each other through every up and down throughout their journey. I want that kind of love and support when I find my forever person!

When five finally rolled around, we were heading out to the track and giving my mom her kiss goodbye. By the time we would be back, she would be asleep, and I wouldn't see her until breakfast the next day. It took about fifteen minutes to get to the track and then another ten minutes to unload the car and tools. We did a once over to make sure the car was ready for hot laps. When we were about done with the car, I saw Chris's truck pull in and park next to us. My heart was racing, not knowing how it would be seeing Jackson for the first time after our argument.

One More Race

I was trying to be inconspicuous with my rubbernecking. I wanted to know if Jackson was with him right now. Who am I kidding, of course he is, he wouldn't miss a race over a stupid little fight? When they got into their spot the passenger side door of the truck opened and out walked Jackson. Before I could register my body, I was running towards him with my arms stretched out. I jumped up into his arms and gave him the biggest apology hug I could think of doing. I think I might have almost knocked him over with how fast I had run towards him. My head was in the perfect crevice of his neck, and I nuzzled into it.

"I'm so sorry Jackson! Can we please never fight again!"

I could feel his heart beating a million miles a second. I backed up and looked at his face and he looked frozen like he wasn't sure what to do. I reached up and grabbed his face and tilted it down towards me.

"Jackson, please look at me. I'm sorry, okay. I don't like when we have these stupid fights."

I really wanted to say to Jackson, *I love you so much, please don't ever leave me alone.* But those words never left my mouth and no words left Jacksons mouth either because he just stared down at me with hurt in his eyes. I didn't understand what was hurting him so bad. Did he love me just as much as I loved him or was, he is hurting because he thought I was with Andy now.

"Jackson, please say something!"

I Could feel the wetness building at the back of my eyes. I didn't want to cry but the thought of him being this upset with me made me think that

One More Race

our friendship was over. I was right this whole time about myself. I was leading him on, and I bet I was doing the same to Andy too. I get to wrapped up on the attention sometimes, they make me feel like I belong, and I don't get that at school. I don't really get that anywhere, but it ends here, it ends tonight! We are friends, we are all friends and that's all!

Jackson

I didn't know what to do or say when Taylor ambushed me like that. I had this whole apology written out in my head and then it all got flushed down the toilet as soon as she was in my arms. I saw my dad smile as soon as I wrapped my arms around her. He had gone up to Sam and they both walked away leaving us by ourselves yet again. I wish they would stop doing that, it makes it harder for me to stay logical when I'm alone with her. All I see is her when she is this close to me, everything gets blocked out.

Then she apologized to me, and I was frozen. What the hell was she even apologizing for? I was the one that raised their voice and basically told her to screw off. I didn't know how to respond to her, so I stood there like a fucking idiot not saying a word as she was begging me to talk to her. When my mind finally caught up to the situation, I saw that she was on the verge of tears.

"Taylor, please don't cry. I'm sorry too, I shouldn't have raised my voice at you the other night."

I wrap my arms around her tighter and hold her for a minute while she cries. I felt like such an asshole for making her cry twice. I was supposed to make her smile, maybe we weren't made for each other if this is how I make her feel. She finally lifts her head away from my bear hug and smiles at me. Like really smiles, showing her teeth and her beautiful rainbow eyes. I got lost momentarily and I slipped again. Next thing I know, my lips are on hers again, but this kiss felt different than the two second peck at the expo. This one had more meaning to it; it was as if we were giving each other our very last kiss because we knew it couldn't happen again. She wrapped her arms around my neck, and I placed hands on her waist.

It started out innocent but then it became fierce with passion and the next thing I knew I had lifted her up and her legs were wrapped around my waist. I had her backed up against the truck door and I had both my hands on her back side with her hands playing in my hair. Her flower scent was playing all around us and it took everything in me to break our kiss first to get a breath. I didn't resume our kiss because I needed to see her face. To see if that had scared her away even more than me raising my voice at her.

She finally opened her eyes, and she was staring at me. Like really staring at me with something fierce but also longing in her eyes. Our gaze is broken by a clearing of someone's throat and we both turn our heads in that direction. Sam is standing there with both his arms crossed and looking furious. I slowly put Taylor down and started to profusely apologize and tell him that it was nothing more than a kiss. I could feel Taylor staring at me when I explained that it was just a kiss, nothing more than that. I didn't know how to deescalate the situation by pleasing them both. *You fucked up good this time Jackson!*

Alycia Carosella

"Jackson, if you wouldn't mind leaving so I could speak with my daughter please!"

He gave me the death glare and all I could do was nod and walk away feeling guilty for getting her in trouble. I should be the one getting yelled at, not her. I'm beginning to think that my body is out to sabotage me. My brain is always telling me to be happy with just friends, but my heart is telling me a completely different story. I decide to leave the trailer and go seek out Andy, so I don't look like a complete loner walking around. It's no surprise that I found Bethany at his trailer with him. If I wasn't mistaken, I would say that she had a thing for him. Poor girl doesn't realize that he is completely head over heels for Taylor. This is quite the love fuck up we are all in, isn't it?

One More Race

"What was that buddy?" Oh, shit did I say that aloud? *Back pedal Jackson, Back pedal!*

"I didn't say anything." *Smooth dipshit.* As soon as I say that my phone vibrates.

Taylor: Hey where did you go? You ditched me.

She seems a bit to chipper for someone who just got caught making out with their best friend.

Jackson: I'm over at Andy's trailer, you should come over. Your best friend Bethany is here smooching up on him.

I see the three dots appear and then disappear.

Taylor: Come back to the truck

Taylor: Please!

I don't bother replying because I'm back at the truck within seconds. I see Taylor still standing right where I left her and then Sam is getting ready for his hot laps. He waves me toward him, and I almost shit my pants. I've never been so scared in my entire life.

"I'm going to tell you what I told Taylor. You both are too young to screw up your life. Kissing is one thing, but that leads to other things and as much as I love you like my own son Jack. I won't let my daughter end up pregnant dropping out of school. You understand where I'm coming from right?"

"Yes, sir. We weren't having sex or even thinking about that I assure you sir." I don't think I've ever called anyone sir before this conversation, I'm just so damn nervous.

"You guys have been friends for a while, let's keep it that way." I don't say another word as he puts on his helmet and gets into the car. I just nod in response to show him that I understand. I turn back towards Taylor, and I can see the shock on her face that her dad just did that. I can't help but think about what he said. Did he really think that I would mess up Taylor's life like that? She is going to be a freshman; I wasn't even thinking about having sex with her. It was just making out and nothing else. Maybe he is right though, maybe friends are all we should be, so mistakes don't happen, and people don't get hurt.

"Taylor, I need…" Before I can finish my sentence Taylor moves up to kiss my lips, but I dodge it the last second.

Taylor

Wow, okay he just backed away from my kiss. I don't know if I should feel hurt or betrayed or embarrassed, but right now I'm feeling all the above.

"Okay so it's okay for you to kiss me, but when I am the one initiating it, you don't want it?"

"Taylor, you know it's not that way at all. We need to talk about this." He gestured between us with his hands.

"What is there to talk about? You kissed me twice now. Doesn't that count for something?"

"We are friends Taylor, which complicates things sometimes. That's all it is, please don't make it any more than it is. You are my best friend, and I can't picture my life without you in it."

"Don't you think that is a sign that we are supposed to be…" He doesn't even let me finish my sentence before cutting me off.

"No Taylor, we can't be anything but friends. I'm sorry if I led you on, that wasn't my intention at all. Please forgive me if I did." His response cracked my heart right open, and it was slowly getting bigger with each passing moment that he didn't take it back. I swallow my pride because I've cried enough in front of this man, and I refuse to do it again.

"Okay Jackson. I understand!" I give him a fake as shit smile and try my best to move on with the moment.

"Let's go find Andy and find a good spot to watch my dad and Chris."

"Yeah sure, let's do it!"

We found Andy with Bethany of course, they were standing in turn one waiting for the race to start. Andy spotted me over his shoulder, and he waved to us to come over. At that moment I was so grateful for him being there by my side. Maybe I don't need to make the decision for myself, I think Jackson just made it for me. We all sat there the whole race and I couldn't help but notice the number of times Bethany tried to steal Andy's attention off me and on to her. If I wasn't mistaken, I would say that Bethany has a little crush on Andy.

One More Race

The thought of flirting with him right now crosses my mind just to spite her for being rude to me last week, but I decided against it. After the heat is done and our dads come back in, Jackson heads back over to the trailer but I stay with Andy. Bethany eventually leaves and then it's just Andy and I hanging out. The way I feel with Andy is how I picture two friends to feel like, but with Jackson it's so different. Andy takes my hand and walks around the pits to show me the race cars. I spot the sprint cars towards the back of the pits. I jump to try to see them, and Andy laughs at me.

"What? I'm short, I need to see those. They are my favorite!"

"What are you waiting for then, let's go!" We headed towards them, and I could feel my heart racing the closer I got to them. These cars right here are my dream, I want to race these big boys.

"I'll own one of these someday!" I could feel Andy smiling at me, so I looked up to him from the car and smiled back at him.

"I can picture you in one of those. You always liked going fast, these suit you so well!" I can't help but hug him at that moment. He doesn't always say the right things but when he does, they are always at the perfect timing.

The rest of the heats go by in a flash, then its feature time! We make our way back to my dad's trailer and see if they need any help with anything. I see Jackson making his way towards us and I brace myself for his cocky response, but it never comes.

"Where did you guys go? I couldn't find you."

"We went to look at the cars."

"Correction, we went to look at my future car."

Andy laughed but Jackson looked confused. I felt bad that he didn't know what we were talking about, but it was his choice to not stay with us.

"What future car? Your sprint car?" My heart tugs a little more at the fact that he remembered the car I wanted when we got older. It's like he knows all the perfect spots to poke tonight to make me feel worse.

"Exactly, maybe in a few years I'll have one of my own." I nod towards my dad, and he laughs.

"Maybe, we will see what your mother says about that."

"What about you Andy, what's your dream race car?"

"I'm not sure to be honest. I've been thinking about trying out asphalt tracks instead of dirt. You know, change it up a bit." I could see Jackson look at

Alycia Carosella

Andy and then back at me assessing my reaction to his answer.

"What about you man, what's your dream car?" I already know his answer is going to be a big block just like his dad. He always told me that he wants to be just like his dad.

"A big block" He slaps his hand on the back of his dad's car and then smiles up at us. I can't help but stare at him and think about all our futures and just hope that we stay in each other's lives that long.

One More Race

Taylor

The summer went by so damn fast, and I was expecting it to be awkward every time I saw Jackson, but it was as if nothing had changed. We were good at that, pretending things weren't there. I became a lot closer to Andy this summer, which was a shocking surprise. Even though we have been friends for a while, I didn't know too much about his family. I found out that he had an older sister and that his parents were divorced, and he lived with his father. He still seems happy though which is a substantial difference if I compare him to Jackson and his mother's relationship.

    We talked about his mom so much back then and I never really liked her. How could you up and leave your husband and kid behind just to pursue your dream? I understand having dreams and wanting to chase them, but you made a commitment to be a wife and more importantly, a mother! Maybe Chris wasn't as supportive as he should have been, but that would only justify the divorce. Not the abandonment of her own child. I wonder if that is why Jackson is so dead set on being friends, he's scared of commitment.

    Jokes on him because if we both don't meet someone by twenty-five, we are getting married. I chuckle thinking about that pact, I wonder if he still remembers that. I think we were nine when we

One More Race

made that, gosh we were so young. I remember the countless times I beat his ass when we would race. Every time there could be a race between us, I ask for it, just one more race. Rather it was on our bicycles or running or now with our karts, eventually with our big cars. I have no doubt that Jackson will be in my life for the rest of my life, whether its friends or lovers.

"You got everything ready for school tomorrow honey?"

"Yes, mom. All good!" I finish getting ready for bed and lay in bed not tired at all.

Taylor: Hey goons, you ready for school tomorrow?

Andy: Yes, you nervous at all with it being your first day of high school?

It's weird not having Jackson be the first one to reply like he always does, but it's whatever.

Jackson: You both will be fine. They make it seem scarier than it really is.

Sometimes I forget that Jack is a year ahead of us and a year older than me.

Andy: I'm exhausted though so sorry for not staying up and talking. I'm heading to bed, goodnight, guys.

Makes sense, Andy seems like a guy who would be asleep by nine and its going on ten thirty right now.

Taylor: Goodnight Andy, I'll text you tomorrow to check in to make sure the seniors don't get you lol.

Taylor: Good luck tomorrow Jackson! Even though it's not your first day of high school, it's still the first day of a new year.

One More Race

Jackson: Goodnight, man, I'll probably see you in the halls. Thank Tay, I appreciate that. I'm going to head to bed too goodnight.

Taylor: Goodnight Jack!

I plug my phone in and set it on my nightstand. I roll over and surprisingly fall right asleep. Here's to new beginnings and new friends. I got woken up around two in the morning and for the life of me have no idea why. Maybe I was snoring so loud it startled me, unfortunately I got the snoring from my dad. Thankfully, the boys don't know or else they would probably give me shit for it. I try to lay back down and go to sleep but my body is betraying me now. I roll over and grab my phone, I get on Facebook and scroll through the feed. Everyone is talking about going to school tomorrow, well technically today. Then I got an idea, I pulled up my messenger app and typed in Jackson's name.

Taylor: One more race?

Taylor: Technically it's morning so good morning...I win

I put a winky kiss emoji at the end of the last message and started to panic that it was a bad idea, but it's too late for it now. I won this race for now, we always text each other good morning and since he is always up before me, he always wins. Not this time Jackson Ford!

One More Race

Jackson

Waking up was a challenge, starting school is always depressing for me. Summer is always my happy spot, being able to race and be with Taylor. That doesn't matter anymore though because this summer changed us. It feels the same sometimes for us when we just hang out in the garage, but it gets so hard for me sometimes to suppress my feelings for her. I just keep replaying Sam's words in my head when that happens, and I usually snap back to reality.

As I'm getting dressed, I see the light flashing on my phone that I have a notification. I unlock it and see the text from Taylor, of course she would try to beat my good morning text. She always says she is going to but always sleeps until the last minute. My body is programmed to be up at six every morning whether I want to or not, so that helps. I can't help but smile at her message and text her back even though she will most likely be out cold.

Jackson: Good Morning Sunshine, looks like you finally did it!

Jackson: don't count on it happening again little lady

Time to get on the grind to get another year down for school. I'm so close to being done and I can't wait. Next year I get to start Boces and get certified to work on cars when I graduate. Taylor and I both said we would open our own garage once we graduated, but I'm not sure that she would still want that with me now.

    I ruined our friendship with those kisses, but with everything in me I can't say that I regret them fully. I hate how it made us afterward, but it just solidified my love for her, yes, I said love! I love Taylor Nicole Martin! I just need to wait for the right time. Maybe if we are serious and when we are older, Sam won't be so worried about us. I mean we both have goals and I think they are close to similar so we would be perfect for each other when it came to pushing toward them.

    I'm hoping this school year will give us a clean slate to start over next summer. Kind of like a buffer, but I need something to distract me from

Alycia Carosella

wanting to talk to her all day and wanting to see her every weekend. Maybe even consider a sport. I laugh at that thought, the only sport I love is racing. I can't picture myself playing or doing anything else.

I make my way through the kitchen and pour myself a cup of coffee. My dad is awake scrolling through his phone.

"Are you all ready? I figured I would drop you off today instead of taking the bus."

I touch my backpack and nod at him.

The day goes by so fast, mainly because we don't really do much on our first day besides introducing ourselves. It's so repetitive and annoying to be honest, I don't care if they know anything about me. I don't want any new friends, we added Andy to our friend group and look where

One More Race

that got us. I can't help but compare my other relationship last to Mine and Taylor's anyway. Our friendship is what everyone wants. I don't want people thinking they would ever become more important of a person than she is in my life. I'll lay low like I always do and go through the motions. One more year closer to being able to be with Taylor for real!

Taylor

These past few months have gone by in a flash, and I even made a new friend which is exciting. Especially since she is my neighbor, and of course she is a girl. I've never really gotten along with girls before, so I was relieved when we hit it off. We hangout all the time talking about her two older sisters and my family. We've grown close for just a few months. I mentioned the boys to Macy, but I didn't want to lay the whole truth on her yet.

One More Race

She lets me nerd out about the cars, and she even comes over and helps me in the garage sometimes. She was exactly what I told myself I needed this year. Maybe everything will fall back into place this summer. Nothing seems to have changed with the boys either, well with Jackson I should say. Andy has been messaging me outside the group chat for once which was a surprise. We've been giving each other updates on school and basically counting down the days until summer again.

His dad has taken him to a few races that are farther away, and I was super jealous. Sometimes I think it would be nice to be with Andy. I mean he is super sweet, he is into the same things as me and his family is put together, so it wouldn't be hard to achieve our dreams. That's if we worked out for the long haul of course. He told me that he wants to go to college to work on race cars and I thought that was typical for him. We all want the same end goal, but if college is in the cards for someone then go for it. I just don't see it making sense for me personally with how much it cost.

I mean we all know the basics, so we just need the certification, and of course the money to open the garage after graduation. Maybe Andy would want to go in with Jackson and I in the garage. I don't get to start Boces until eleventh grade though, so I have some time. I feel the vibration of my phone in my pocket.

Macy: SOS

Taylor: on my way

One More Race

When I get to her doorway, I don't even have time to knock before she is pulling me inside towards her bedroom.

"What's the sos for?" She turns towards me and shows me her phone. There's a thread of messages from Cody Solomon. He is our star basketball player and apparently has a thing for Macy. Makes sense, she is gorgeous with her long black hair and piercing blue eyes. Her eyes aren't dark like Jackson's, but they are a light blue that reminds me of diamonds with the way they sparkle in the light. The darkness of her hair helps make them pop. She is taller than me and is toned like an athlete.

When I first met her, I was jealous, because she is absolutely stunning, and I was just…me. I always say that I'm going to get in shape, but then never do. I've just started calling myself thick and trying to accept my body for what it is. At Least being on the bigger side has gifted me with a fuller chest than most girls my age. I've always had self-image problems and I think that's why I never really put myself out there, but I also always had Jackson. He was always there to remind me that I was enough and then Andy started doing the same. After reading all the messages I turn to her and ask her what's the problem.

"He seems interested in you. What's the problem with that?"

"He is the most popular guy in school, and I'm not, it doesn't add up!"

"Then ask him why he likes you?" I shrug it off like she is being over dramatic, if you want to know how someone is feeling you just have to be honest with them. After thinking that, Jackson pops into my head. We both have been teetering on the line of honesty when it came to admitting to our feelings for each other.

"I don't know Taylor; I don't think it's that easy."

"Yeah, I get that. I don't know, maybe just go for it but keep your guard up so you don't get hurt."

She looks all giddy with the idea of going for Cody and I can't help but feel excited for her but also a little bit jealous. I want to feel excited about someone wanting me like that. I felt like that the night Jackson kissed me at the track. I still don't understand what switch got flipped in him to suddenly not want me after that kiss. It was everything I ever imagined it would be and then when I finally had the courage to keep going, he chops me down.

"Any progress on your end?"

"What do you mean?" I have a feeling she is talking about Andy because I talk to him more than Jackson now and he has been dropping hints of wanting to ask me out.

"With Andy...duh."

"Umm I don't know to be honest. He acts like he wants more than friendship but I'm not sure if it's in the cards for us."

"He obviously likes you more than friends from what you've told me. Do you feel the same?" I swallow hard at that question because I'm so torn about it. At the beginning of last summer, I would have said no, but he is starting to grow on me. I've been trying really hard to not compare him to Jack, but it comes and goes, but maybe this is what I need to fully get over Jack. I need to convince my head that we are just friends and will always ever be friends.

"Yeah, I think so."

"Then go for it girl. Life's too short for what ifs." I rolled my eyes because she was literally freaking out about this same thing a few moments ago. It's as if she can read my mind because she starts laughing as soon as I do.

"I think you're right, let's do this!"

Alycia Carosella

Jackson

The last few months of school we finished so fast I don't even remember most of it except for Taylor. She started to act weird towards me that last month of school, but I never confronted her about it. Maybe it was because of our camping trip coming up this summer. I forgot that my dad had planned a trip up to Old Forge and I invited Taylor to come along. Or maybe it was just that summer was approaching and she was nervous about seeing me again, period. We had only seen each other a few times throughout the school year on the weekends when my dad had gone over to Sam's house. We both started to paint our bodies for the karts this year. Taylor really is talented with her artistic side! My dad never brings up the kiss I had with Taylor, so I don't know if he knows about the second one or if he is just oblivious to it.

Either way I'm fine with pretending it didn't happen when I'm around Sam. I want him to know that I took his words to heart and that I'm taking my relationship with Taylor seriously. This last class is dragging on and it's killing me. I just want to get my hands on the cars and see Taylor again. The anticipation is killing me, then I feel my phone vibrate and I see a text from my dad.

Alycia Carosella

Dad: I'm out front. We've got a lot of work to do to get the cars ready, so we need to go straight to Sam's.

Jackson: Sounds good. See you in a few.

Dad: Get off your phone in class, mister!

I muffle my laughter at my father trying to be stern with me. If he's being serious then he would be pissed at all the times I've spent texting Taylor throughout class. The bell finally rings and then my sophomore year is in my rear view. I see my dad's truck as soon as I walk outside and can't help but power walk to it. I can't wait to see Taylor.

"How was your last day?"

"Same as always. One less year down until graduation." My dad sighs at my response.

One More Race

"Don't be so dang eager to grow up on me kid." He nudges my shoulder and smiles at me. Then he pulls off and we are headed for Taylor's.

As soon as we pull in, I go to see if she is in the garage, but she isn't, so I make my way into the house to find her. I'm greeted by Taylor's mom Julia, and she tells me that she is next door. I scrunch my eyebrows together in confusion.

"Next door?"

"Yes honey, she is friends with the new neighbor Macy."

"Oh okay, thank you Mrs. Martin!" She nods in my response but I'm out the door before she can say your welcome.

I make my way over and I see Taylor standing next to this tall girl with jet black hair and wow her eyes are hypnotizing. She's still not as pretty as my Taylor with her rainbow eyes though. I can see that she knows I'm behind her because her shoulder starts to tense, and I can see the goosebumps on her arms.

"Hey Tay!" She turns with a smile, but not her real smile. She looks nervous for some reason, and I feel that now is the best time to confront this head on. She has been acting weird for weeks now.

"Hey Jackson, I didn't even realize you were at my house. This is my friend Macy."

"Correction, her best friend!" She laughs at her remark, but it lights a fire under my skin.

"No, that would be me, I'll always be the best friend no matter what." I see Taylor slowly close her eyes and swallow hard.

"Alright we'll I'll be over in a second Jack. I just need to talk to Macy."

One More Race

"Did I do something wrong? again?" I see Taylor let out a long breath and then look at Macy, I can see that Macy is confused and mouths 'again' to Taylor. Maybe she hasn't told Macy about me or told her about our kisses, both of our first kisses. "I'm dating Andy…" wow okay that came out blunt and punched me right in the gut, but what was I expecting. I had rejected her last summer and she deserved to be happy, maybe she was with him.

"Oh, okay that makes sense."

"What do you mean it makes sense?"

"Listen Tay, he obviously had a thing for you. It was so clear with the way he was making passes at you. All I care about is that you're happy. I'll always be here, remember, the two of us forever"

"Yeah."

"Well now that we got that out of the way, can you stop acting weird towards me now?" I can see her expression soften after we have crossed that bridge together.

"Yeah, of course. Umm I'll be over in a second okay." I nod and turn back towards her house clutching my chest trying to make sure my heart is still in the spot it should be. Because it feels like it just turned into liquid and seeped out of my body. I don't know why I thought this wasn't coming. She wasn't going to just sit around and wait for me like I am for her. Timing must be perfect for us to be together.

One More Race

Taylor

I can't believe the cat is finally out of the bag about Andy and me. It feels good to have it out there and be honest with Jack but the look on his face made me feel like shit. Our camping trip should be interesting in a few weeks. Macy was there the whole time and it made me feel even more embarrassed. I still hadn't told her about the kisses with Jackson. I wasn't ready to bring those memories back up yet if I was being honest with myself. The last kiss had been phenomenal, and I

One More Race

wanted more, but obviously Jackson just wanted to be friends. So, I need to move on with someone else, with Andy.

Thankfully, Jackson was his amazing self and still is willing to be my friend. I didn't doubt that he wouldn't stick around after I told him, but the nervousness was there. That's one thing I adore about him, he is nothing like his mother. He has always been there for me and continues to be an I couldn't ask for a better best friend!

"Wow, that was something."

"I'm sorry Macy"

"He clearly loves you, Taylor."

Wait did I hear her correctly, did she just say Jackson loves me? Well obviously, we love each other but only as friends.

"What! No, he doesn't. We're just friends."

"Taylor, the way he looked at you was clearly with love. He was so heart broken when you told him about you and Andy."

"Way to make me feel like an ass Mac."

"I'm sorry, I'm just stating the obvious. What did he mean when he said, again?" I sigh at her question but decide that now is a suitable time to come clean about Jack.

"We've kissed before, twice actually. My dad caught us the second time and we haven't really been normal after that."

"Dang that explains the look then."

"What do you mean?"

"He's scared of your dad, so he is keeping his distance from you. What did your dad say to you guys after he saw you?"

One More Race

"I don't know what he said to Jackson, he spoke to us separate. As soon as he caught us, he told Jackson to basically beat it so he could let into me. All he did was preach about how I was young and needed to think before acting and to stay focused on my future."

"The normal dad speech I guess, I just assumed he said the same to Jackson." I could see Macy raise her eyebrows and at that moment I was curious and dumbstruck. Why hadn't I asked Jackson what my dad said to him in the first place. Now I needed to know what he had said.

"I don't know Tay; it seems to me that he is just listening to your father and doing what he asks. That doesn't mean he still doesn't care for you."

"Damn you Mac, you're supposed to help me make decisions, not confuse me into thinking I made the wrong one." I could see her smirking out of the corner of my eye. I'm glad she is getting amusement out of my miserable love life.

"Sorry love, but I still love you and I support your choice no matter who you choose."

Did I even have a choice at this point? I had been dating Andy for a month now, well I don't know if you would call it dating. We've gone to the movies with some of his other friends and he took me to one of his races. Besides that, we have just been talking over the phone about school and the summer, I haven't even kissed him yet. I can't just drop him because there might be a chance with Jack, can I?

Jesus, no I can't do that to him, it would hurt him too much and we are still friends. I need to see this out with Andy, but still push Jack to see why he distanced himself that night.

When I get back to the garage, I see Jack working on his kart like I didn't just tell him that I have a boyfriend. He turns when I walk near him, and I can feel the hair on the back of my neck stand up with those ocean eyes on me. I haven't been able to just stare into them since that night and I miss getting lost in them. I could go for getting lost right now with how chaotic my thoughts are.

"What are you working on?"

"Just stripping it so I can finally get going the body on. Are you still going painting yours?"

"Absolutely, I'm almost done with it. Want to help?" I can see that there is a smile hidden on his face.

"Yeah sure." I grab his hand and yank him towards the back room in the garage. As soon as we reach the doorway he stops abruptly, he stands in the doorway not going any further. He is just staring at the bodies of our go-karts.

"What do you think? I know I should have asked first, but I was hoping to surprise you with it.'

I see him smiling at both kart bodies I've been working on the past few months. I finished both sketches and then started to paint them. I tried to have them finished for this race season but there are a few more things to add to both.

'You did both?' I nod to his question and smile.

'They aren't finished yet, want to help me finish them?'

'Absolutely, but they might not look as good as they do now with my touch on them.' I laugh at his response because anything looks better than how we got them.

We spend the next few hours painting and our hands are covered in spray paint, and we look ridiculous with these masks on. I can help but laugh when we are done, and I finally get a look at ourselves.

"It's that bad?' I pull the mask down and turn towards Jackson.

'No, we just look ridiculous.' He starts laughing and points to my nose.

'Told you we look ridiculous.' I see him shaking his head and trying to stop laughing so he can talk.

"You have a mark over your nose that looks like you took off your snore nose strip." He is holding his stomach because he is laughing so hard.

"For your information, I do not snore Mr. Ford!"

His face is turning red and it's the opposite of the variations of blues all over his hands. He tilts his head back because he is laughing so hard.

"If you say so Tay."

"What does that mean?" He is smirking trying to subside his laughter and that's when he looks me straight in the eyes with that ocean of his.

"Who do you think took you to bed the night you fell asleep watching The Evil Dead?" He lets his smile come through.

"You are most definitely a snorer young lady!"

What is happening here? He put me in my bed that night? Wait did my dad know and that was why he was laughing the morning after?

One More Race

"I didn't realize you were the one to put me in my bed that night. Thanks!" I try not to dwell on it longer than I should, but my mind has other plans.

"No problem, I won't tell a sole, scouts honor." He puts two fingers to his chest and then raises them, I can't help but laugh at him because he has never been in the boy scouts ever. I could not picture him doing anything like that.

"You were never in the boy scout's you goon." He pulls me into a hug and we both laugh together. There it is again, that feeling where nothing else matters except for Jackson and me.

"Okay so let's finish these!"

"What do you mean? They are finished."

I see him reach for an actual can of paint and a paint brush. He makes his way over to me and reaches for my hand and starts placing paint on it. Then he does the same to himself and places his hand on my kart body right towards the back of it.

"There, now when we are out on the track you know I'll always be with you, helping push you towards that finish line."

I smile, but all I want to do is leap into his lap and steal another kiss from him. I wish he would explain why friends is all that is on the table for us. I go to his Kart and do the same. We both step back and look at them together.

"You were right, now they are finished!"

We both look at each other and hug, probably for longer than necessary, but it was long overdue. I can't help but feel my insides warm with his big arms wrapped around me. He breaks the hug first and I long for his warm embrace as soon as it breaks. I need to get my head straight, I'm with

One More Race

Andy and before I continually try to get Jacksons attention I need to figure out if seeing Andy is what I truly want. *Pick one Taylor! You can't have both...* I wish the universe would just make the decision for me because I want them both!

Taylor

Talking to Andy isn't the same as talking with Jackson. When we talk about our dreams, I can't picture any of mine with him in it as my person. I always placed Jackson there and lately it has just been me. Maybe I'm meant to be alone, and Jackson is meant to be with someone else. I feel awful for not telling Andy that my heart still feels for Jack, but he would think that I didn't care for him at all if I told him that. At first, I was hoping to make

One More Race

Jackson wake up by being with Andy, but I ended up having fun with Andy. Well until Jackson invaded my thoughts again.

He always ruined my happiness with anyone else. Who am I kidding, he is my happiness, he always has been and always will be! I need to tell Andy that I can't be with him. I can't go this whole summer lying to myself about who makes me truly happy. First things First, I need to know what my father said to Jackson to get him to back off so much.

We had finished the Karts a week ago and packed the trailer this morning, so we were ready for tonight's race. My father has no excuse to not entertain my questioning. When I spot him getting ready outside near the truck, I swallow the lump in my throat and make my way towards him. He turns towards me and smiles at me and it makes me more nervous than I was to begin with.

"You ready to head out little girl?"

"I'm far from a little girl dad." I could see his smile falter as we got into the truck to head out. I sat in the passenger side seat looking out the window for a while before I built up enough courage to just come out with it.

"What did you say to Jackson?" My father slowly turned his head and furrowed his brows trying to understand what I meant.

"What do you mean sweetheart?"

"The night you caught us Kissing, what did you say to him when you talked to him?" He let out a big breath and opened his mouth to start talking but I cut him off.

One More Race

"It's just…after that night he hasn't really been acting the same towards me and I thought it was just because of the…umm…kiss. He is my best friend dad, I love him."

I can see the defeat in his face when I finally let him talk.

"I told him the same thing I told you, to focus on the future."

"Is that it? Because I don't think he would have been acting like this if that was all you said to him?" My dad looks embarrassed for what he is about to say, and I try to brace myself.

"I might have told him that I didn't want my daughter to end up pregnant and dropping out of school." He drops his head down and I can't help but gasp. I don't know if I'm embarrassed that my father acted like that or furious because he doesn't think we are responsible enough to know not to have that happen. We both have goals we want to carry out before having kids and they are going to happen. Jackson was my biggest supporter for the garage and then he started to pull away from me. "Dad, I love you, but that was out of line. If you truly trust me then you should know that I wouldn't let that happen. Neither would Jackson, we both have plans for our future and he always pushed me to do my best."

"Plus, I haven't even had sex yet." I can see him shiver went the word sex left my mouth.

"Okay, I get what you're saying. I just knew that he was the one to put you in bed the night you were watching movies and then I caught you kissing. I was caught off guard and I might have come off a

One More Race

little too hard on him, but I just want both of you to be safe okay." He hesitates with his next statement. "Do I need to talk to your mother about birth control?" I can tell how uncomfortable he is with this discussion, but I am so grateful that he is talking about it with me and wanting to be proactive. I reach across the middle seat and give him a squeeze hug.

"I love you so much dad."

"I love you to sweetie, so…is that a, yes?" I can't help but laugh because he is still hung up on the birth control thing. I mean it wouldn't hurt to be on it for when the time comes but I don't plan on having sex anytime soon. I only want to be with Jackson, and he acts like he isn't interested in me anymore.

"Can you talk to him please? Maybe apologize for coming off too strong? I want us to go back to normal and I think he fears you." We both laugh because my dad doesn't look scary at all, but I can see how Jack would be afraid of him. Especially If he wanted to show him that he was a practical choice for his daughter. Operation get Jackson back is in full swing. Tonight, should be interesting especially since I haven't seen Andy since I told him that I wanted to just be friends. He was extremely understanding about it, I think it was because we weren't really involved in the first place. I didn't tell him that I left him because my heart was with someone else, but It's pretty clear that it's the case. I really am blessed to have two great friends in my life!

One More Race

Jackson

I can't wait to be on the track tonight and to let off some steam. Ever since Tay told me she was with Andy; I couldn't stop thinking about them together. Wondering if he had kissed her yet or put his hands anywhere on her body. To say I was jealous was an understatement and seeing them tonight is going to be rough. It will all be better once I'm out on the track.

Once we pulled up next to Sam's truck, I scanned around for Taylor but came up empty handed. I was both disappointed and relieved at the same time. I started to unload the truck and then Sam called my name. I looked behind me and saw that he was over near his truck giving me a smile.

"Do you mind if I could talk to you for a minute?" I look over to my dad nervously, but he just shrugs his shoulders and tilts his head in Sam's direction.

"Uh yeah sure." I make my way over to him and my legs feel like noodles so I'm not sure how I made it over here so gracefully.

"What can I do for you Sam?"

"I need to apologize to you!" I try to think back on something that he would need to apologize to me for and I come up empty.

"I don't understand, what are you apologizing for?"

"I shouldn't have come at you as hard as I did when I caught you and Taylor kissing. Obviously, Taylor cares for you a lot. I just want to make sure both of you are being careful and thinking of consequences before jumping into anything."

I don't know what to say to him and before I can say anything my arms are wrapped around his body into a hug. I feel relieved that he doesn't hate me, but that doesn't change the fact that Tay and I aren't even together, so he has nothing to worry about. "You don't know how much I appreciate your apology Mr. Martin, but Taylor and I are just friends. You don't have to worry about anything."

"I'm going to give this to you straight Jackson, you guys are getting older. I'm not saying that you guys are old enough to do things like…sex, but I see the way you guys look at each other. Just because you aren't adults yet doesn't mean you don't love each other. I knew at your age that I loved Julia. I'm just saying that if you guys do take the friendship to something else that I'm okay with that as long as you guys are smart about it." I still am trying to register what he just said but when it all comes together, and I smile.

"Thanks Sam, you have no idea how much that means to me."

"Of course, Jack, I'm proud of you both." He wraps his arms around me, and we hug again.

I'm overwhelmed with emotions after that talk with Sam, so I decide to do what Taylor would do, music therapy. I get in my dad's truck and turn on my Spotify and close my eyes. I must have been so zoned into the music because I didn't even hear the truck door open and for someone to get inside. The song ends and the next song comes on and I swear it's like fate, until I open my eyes and turn to see Taylor in the passenger side of my dad's truck.

One More Race

Maybe it's still fate because she is here right in front of me and has been this whole time. I point to the radio, and she smiles.

"Did you put this on?"

"It's kind of our song so how couldn't I?" I don't want to ruin our moment, but I need to know about Andy and if they are still together, to see if I even have a shot at being Taylors man.

"What about you and Andy?" She lets out a long breath and bites her bottom lip.

"We broke up, well I broke up with him. He's not you Jackson, I thought I could be with someone who isn't you, but you won't stay away." I'm confused by her statement because I've been trying to stay as far away emotionally as I could from her.

"You are always in my head all the time and even when you're not. You're with me in the little things I

Alycia Carosella

do or when I hear a race car engine or when I smell the burning rubber of race car tires. Everything reminds me of you!" I can't help but smile at her. "It's always been us, just you and me! I wanted you then, I want you now, and I want you when we are old. I will always want you, Taylor!"

We both smile with watered eyes, and I bring her in for another kiss, but this time it's different because she is mine and I am hers. Camping next weekend should be fun! We both break our kiss to get ready to go out on the track and kick some ass!

Andy wins the race again, but I end up in second and Taylor ended the race in fifth out of twelve cars. We all are getting better, and I can't help but be proud of all of us. After the race we all huddle at Andy's trailer and celebrate with him on his win. He is surprisingly upbeat for getting broken up with.

"Congrats on yet another win man!" He comes in for a hug and I start to feel nervous that he will know about mine and Taylors kiss earlier. Speaking of Taylor where did she go? We both circle trying to find Taylor and she is talking with Bethany at her trailer. Andy and I share a look of concern, but it soon subsides when they both start laughing with each other.

"Wow, okay I guess they are friends now?" Andy starts laughing at my remark and then leans back on his trailer.

"She is pretty great!" I look at him and he is serious now staring at Taylor.

"Yeah man, she's pretty extraordinary! I'm sorry what happened between you guys."

Alycia Carosella

"I would hardly say we were serious; we just went out a few times. It was more of testing the waters than anything. When she said she wanted to be friends two weeks ago, I was kind of relieved."

Wait did he say two weeks ago? I thought she broke up with him recently.

"Why were you relived?" He puts his arm around my shoulder and chuckles a little. That's when I see Taylor glance at us with a worried look on her face. I smile at her to show her that we are good.

"Because it was never going to work out between us. We're friends, that's all we should be even if I thought I wanted more with her. She loves you; you know that right?" I turn to look at his face and he is smirking at my deer in headlights look.

"Yeah, I love her to man" At this time, I am so damn grateful to have this guy in our friendship. He may have gotten on my nerves, but he looked out for Taylor when I didn't and always assured that she was happy. I couldn't have asked for a better friend than that. I see Taylor hug Bethany and then make her way over to us.

"Take care of her Jack!"

"What are you boys talking about over here."

"We are more interested in what you and Beth were talking about?" She puts her hands on her hips at us dodging her questioning.

"We were just letting each other know how good we both did out there. I finished right behind her, and I was pretty close a few times." Andy and I both smile and look beyond Taylor at Bethany and then back at Taylor.

"That's great, Bethany is really a great girl once you get to know her." I can see a bit of pink flush Andy's cheeks when he says that.

"Well, I just wanted to come congratulate you on another win! You did great out there Andy, hopefully someday I'll get to beat you." We all laugh with Taylor at her remark and Andy gets up to give her a hug.

"You can try, but I wouldn't count on it." He winks at Taylor, and she shakes her head with a smirk. Bethany makes her way over and that is our cue to head back to our trailers too. We both say bye to Andy and Beth and turn to walk away. As we are midway to turned around, I grab Taylors hand and she looks at me in shock that I am doing this in front of everyone, especially Andy. Out of the corner of my eye, I see Andy smiling and then give

One More Race

his full attention to Bethany. Maybe this isn't such a shit show of a love triangle after all.

Alycia Carosella

Taylor

Camping day! I'm still surprised my parents are letting me go camping this whole weekend with Jackson and his dad. We left early this morning since it's a few hours' drive to Old Forge. Jackson and I have been hanging out in the back seat listening to music for most of it. It feels weird to finally call Jackson my boyfriend and be able to have it out in the open now that our parents know. I'm going to be a sophomore this coming falls and Jack is starting his junior year, so we are still young when it comes to dating. I don't think our parents think it's serious, but when I say I love Jackson Dominic Ford, I mean it with all my body, heart, and soul.

    We arrive at the camp site a little after two and we unload the truck and start setting up our tents. We each have our own and Chris has planted his right in between both of ours. He glances at both of us and gives us a wink.

"Just in case you guys get any ideas at night."

Jackson and I share a look and then start laughing at his remark. Once we finish getting set up, we eat and then decide to explore the nature trails. Chris told us to be back for dinner, but that we were free to explore the area.

    We walk the three-mile trail and can see the water park next door in the distance. It looks huge and I can't wait to go tomorrow. Walking with

Jackson with our hands latched together is like heaven. Well, if I knew what heaven was like, I would assume that I feels like this. I feel like we are the only two people on the planet right now and I feel invincible with him by my side. He truly is my kryptonite and I hope he knows how safe he makes me feel.

    We stop in front of a little pond to watch the animals; the water is dark blue with little green pads in it. It makes me want to see those ocean eyes, I turn, and Jackson is already looking at me. I start to blush and then smile at him, then I look into those huge oceans of eyes and I'm floating.

"Do you know how fucking beautiful you are Taylor?" How did I get so lucky to have this man in my life for this long?

One More Race

"Only because you constantly remind me." I kiss his cheek and squeeze his hand a little harder. I rest my head on his should and we go back to watching the animals. I hear him whisper under his breath and I'm not sure if I was meant to hear it or not, but I can't help feeling relieved by his omission. *Because I love you to Jackson Ford*

We must lose track of time because when Jack looks down at his phone it's time to head back for dinner.

"We should start heading back now if we want to make it back in time for dinner." I smirk at him and then push him; I look back and yell.

"One more race? First one back gets the first smore." I wink at him and start running, but I wore my damn Sperry's, and he wins by a long shot. By the time we get back to the campsite we are all out of breath and laughing. Chris is giving us a weird look at us being fools.

"What on earth are you guys doing."

"Racing, like always." Chris shakes his head and we all chuckle and start setting the picnic table up for our burgers.

After dinner we relax by the fire and I take out my notebook and start drawing, Chris is on his hone and Jackson is sitting next to me rubbing my feet soaking up the fire. When I realize Jack isn't rubbing my feet anymore, I look up to see him roasting marshmallows and making smores. I smile and just watch him as the light of the fire emanates his face. Once he gets the smores assembled he gives one to me and we clink them together and say cheers. I see him waiting before digging in to his.

"What are you waiting for?"

One More Race

"For you to take your first bite."

"But you won the race, you are supposed to get the first smore, remember?" We both are smiling, and I can feel Chris's eyes on us at this point. We probably both look like idiots just hold smores in our hands waiting for one another to dig in first.

"It wasn't a fair race; you didn't have proper shoes. So, by default you win this one." I smirk at him and catch a quick glance at Chris, he is looking a Jackson smiling so proud at him. I hope he knows how sweet of a guy he raised. I will forever be grateful to him for bring Jackson into my life!

"I guess I'll allow it this time." I take a bite and a little bit of the graham cracker falls on my paper and I brush it off.

"What are you drawing Taylor?" I'm not self-conscious when it comes to my drawing, but I also don't think it's the best either. I pocket my hesitation and turn my drawing around so they can see it.

"I know it's not the best, but I thought I would be good to have an outline for when it's time to get the garage going." Jackson Smiles at me with his crooked smile, my heart melts.

"I think it looks fantastic! I can't wait to see you kids achieve your goals. I have no doubt that you won't get the garage looking just like that. I'm proud of you both for sticking with your dreams." He doesn't know how much that means to me, for him to not second guess my goals. Jackson brings me into his arms and kisses the top of my head, I pull away after realizing we just ate smores.

"I hope you don't have marshmallow on your face mister, that's a pain to get out of my hair." Both the boys laugh, but they truly don't know how annoy that is to get out. Jackson licks all around his lips and stares at me through the light glow from the fire.

"All clean missy"

It's time to settle into our tents and Chris is the last one to go in, probably to make sure we go into our own tents. I don't blame him, my parents put him in charge of me, so he is being safe. After I say goodnight to Jackson and Chris, I get into my sleeping back and try to fall asleep. It feels like an entire day goes by but when I look at my phone it's only been two hours. I can hear Chris lightly snoring in his tent next to me. I've been tossing and turning this whole time trying to fall asleep, but my body hates me. I know I shouldn't, but I open my tent away to seek out Jackson.

As soon as I start to unzip the tent, he sits right up staring at me with tired eyes.

"What's wrong? Are you okay?" I smile at his response but also feel bad for waking him if he had actually fallen asleep.

"I couldn't sleep, I'm sorry if I woke you. I can go back to my tent if you want me to, I know I shouldn't be in here." He sits up even more and pats down next to him after I finish zipping the tent back up.

"Come here babe." I snuggle in next to him and relax under his warm embrace, I could get use to this. My head is nuzzled into that sweet crevice that I swear was made just for me. I'm listening to his heartbeat faster as we lay there, I shift to get closer to him and that when I feel His erection on my thigh. As if he reads my mind, he tries to push it away from me, but I grab his hand.

"Its fine. Leave it." I look up at his face he is staring into my eyes with so much hunger, I lose my focus on reality. Then our lips are on each other, and he slowly slips on top of me. I welcome him by wrapping my legs around his hips.

We both are panting when we realize that we have taken both of our bottoms off. He looks down at me with serious eyes and I know a question is coming.

"Do you want to? I-I…. uhm…I've never done this before." I don't know why he needed to specify that this is his first time. I never have done this either and to say I was scared was an understatement. My mother hadn't really had the sex talk with me, I found out most things on the internet or school gossip. The one thing my mother told me over and over was that your first time was going to hurt and that has deterred me for this long.

"Nether have I, but yes, I want to. Do you want to? We don't have to if you…" I don't get to finish my sentence because Jackson runs his hand down my cheek and then kisses me softly.

I shift to make room for him down there, but then I hear a rip of a wrapper. *Oh goodness, how did I forget that step, of course, a condom.* Well, that was almost bad, he rolls it on and positions himself above me looking down at my face.

"Are you sure? We don't have to…" I reach for his face and kiss him and then nod my head. He slowly approaches my entrance. He starts to push himself inside, but the pressure is too much, holy hell does it hurt.

One More Race

"Wait, wait!" I start to panic with the amount of pain with just the tip in.

"What's wrong? Does it hurt? We're stopping." He takes the condom off before I can answer him and then wraps me into a hug.

"I'm sorry Jackson." He backs away and looks at my face with concern and kisses my forehead. "There is nothing to be sorry for Taylor, you aren't ready yet. We have all the time in the world to do that, right now I'm fine with just laying with you." I kiss him and lay my head on his chest while he wraps his arms around me. I fall asleep within minutes.

Alycia Carosella

Jackson

I woke up to the smell of flowers and when I looked down, I realized that Taylor had slept in my tent. I had every intention of bring her back to her tent once she passed out, but I must have snoozed off to. I look at the clock on my phone and just like clockwork, its six in the morning. I grab around for my boxers and pants and exit the tent, but not before grabbing the condom and the wrapper. I stuff them in the bottom of the trash and hid them the best I can and then start on making the coffee. I hear

One More Race

rustling in the tent, and I expect it to be my father but when I turn around, to my surprise its Taylor.

Lord have mercy, can this girl get any more perfect! He hair is all messy from sleeping and she definitely looks like she could have had more sleep, but hell she is still the most beautiful girl I've ever seen.

"Good morning, Sweetheart." She smiles at me and my whole body warms up, I go over to her and plant a kiss on her forehead.

"How did you sleep?" She sits down at the picnic table and runs her hands over her arms like she is chilly.

"Good after I was in your arms." I will have her in my arms for the rest of our damn life if that's what she needs.

"I'm glad I could help" I wink at her and her expression changes to worry.

"I'm sorry again about last night Jack, I just…" I set down a cup of coffee in front of her and sit next to her. I take her face in my hands and kiss her forehead.

"You don't need to apologize for anything." I kiss her nose next.

"You did nothing wrong; we have time baby." I kiss both of her cheeks next.

"Remember, it's you and me forever!" I kiss her mouth next and what comes out of her mouth after that last kiss is my new favorite sound from Taylor. She's looking at me assessing my reaction to the L word and I know that the smile on my face is the indication she was looking for.

One More Race

"I love you to Taylor, I always have!" After that comes out of my mouth, I hear the zipper on my dad's tent.

"You guys are up early, how did you guys' sleep?" Taylor looks at me and smirks.

"Good, do you want coffee?" I see my dad's eyes light up at the mere mention of coffee. I hand him the mug and sit next to Taylor.

"So what time are we heading out today for our festivities?" My dad sits across from us at the table and sips his coffee.

"The park doesn't open until eight this morning, so I figured we would eat breakfast and then head over there for the day. Bring sunscreen because it's supposed to be hot today." Taylor nods and we all chit chat for a bit while drinking our coffee.

Alycia Carosella

"Want to play cards?" I turn towards Taylor and nod with a smirk, I always beat her at cards, but she continues to try to win.

"What are we playing? Thirty-one again?"

"Of course, what else would we play?" I laugh and wait for her to deal the cards. My dad gets started on breakfast in the background.

We play a few hands before breakfast is ready and surprisingly Taylor won both hands. Either she's been practicing, or she cheated! We eat breakfast and then its time to get ready. We all head back to our tents to get our swimsuits on under our clothes and then we are off to the park for the day. Once we arrive, there aren't that many people, so the lines aren't long at all.

"Alright, so I don't plan on going on the rides. So, I'm trusting you guys to stick together. We will be

One More Race

meeting at this giant lumber jack statute at twelve to check in and figure out lunch. If you need me before then, just call me." I look over at Taylor and she looks so excited to be able to spend the day with just us.

"Got it!" Before my dad can say another word, I grab Taylors hand and pull her towards the rides. I span my hands across the park to display the rides like I'm advertising.

"Pick a ride, any ride!" I see a smirk forming on her face as she is looking at the rides. She points to the bumper cars, and I can't help but feel a sense of pride that out of all the rides, she chooses that one.

"I see you want to lose today Ms. Martin."

"I'm not sure about that one Mr. Ford, I won cards this morning. The tables are finally turning for me. One more race?"

Alycia Carosella

"Always, Let's go!" We get in line and as soon as its our time to get in, we pick our cars on opposite sides of the track. I can see the determination in her eyes to win at this, but she is going down. As soon as the buzzer goes, we start to chase after one another. There are a bunch of little kids on the ride to, so we have to take it easy. I look eyes with Taylor and tell her I'm coming for her, but I fail to see this little snot face boy who just runs into my side pushing me out of the clear shot to get Taylor. She starts bursting out into laughter and I can't help but stare at how beautiful she is and just listen to her voice.

We finally are lined up and go full on chicken with it, hitting each other head on. We both jerk in the cars and start laughing. We get each other a few other times before the bell rings again and the cars stop moving. As we get outside the ride we are still laughing, and I pull her in for a kiss. "Gosh I love you, marry me right now!" I haven't actually come out and said that to her like this and it feels so good to be able to. Of course, I'm not actually proposing for real, but I have no doubts that I will someday. I can't picture my life with anyone else! She stops laughing and nudges my shoulder with a smile.

"I love you to Jackson, but let's hold on the proposal until after high school mister."

We go on so many more rides throughout the day and it has to be the best day of my damn life. I will never forget this day! Heading back home before starting school is going to be rough after how eventful this summer has been.

Alycia Carosella

Taylor

This whole summer was a blast, and I don't think anyone could convince me otherwise. I got everything I ever wanted and then some. Camping with Jackson and his dad was so much fun besides that damn sunburn we ended up getting. Racing that following week sucked, even though I applied sunscreen I had gotten double sunburn and thought I was going to die. Of course, Jackson got burnt and then had this beautiful tan afterwards. I was

One More Race

extremely jealous, but I also wasn't complaining because hot damn did that tan compliment his abs.

    Today is the first day of my sophomore year and all I can think about is Jackson. He started a new job already, its minimum wage but its still money. I don't mind him having one, but damn does it make it hard to plan time together. I know we should be focusing on school, but with him doing that, Boces and a job this year, I'm put on the back burner for now. It sucks but I'm willing to sacrifice less time with him if it helps him achieve his goals. That's what friends are for and what girlfriends are supposed to do right? I have a lot of advanced classes this year, so its looking like I can double up and maybe graduate early next year.

    The first day always go by so quick, I think its because you do absolutely nothing but introduce yourself and then get handed homework. My class has been the same since middle school, so the introductions are always the same. Thankfully, Macy is in majority of my classes this year. I haven't made any other friends in school; I wouldn't really count Cody since he is just a branch off of Macy. He surprisingly is a really chill guy though; I was so happy when she told me that they decided to try the dating game. Cody reminds me of Jackson a little with the way he profusely protects Macy. A double date is in our future, that's if Jackson ever gets a day off.

Macy: What are your plans for tomorrow? I have like three study halls.

Taylor: I have a meeting with my advisor at the end of the week to discuss my schedule. I think they are going to let me double up and maybe do Boces this year.

Macy: I thought that was for juniors and up?

Taylor: I'm taking junior classes this year too. What electives did you choose?

Macy: I only got to choose two, I got stuck with home economics because cooking was full and then I'm taking a sculpture class. What about you?

Taylor: Photography and Sculpture. I can't wait to start them both. I have to go; I finally have dinner with Jackson tonight and I need to get ready. Ill see you tomorrow love you!

Macy: Get it girl! Love you to!

I shake my head at my phone and start picking out an outfit for our date tonight. I'm not sure where we are going, but my birthday is in a few weeks so I'm guessing its for that. As soon as I finish getting ready, I hear my mother yell for me and tell me that Jackson is here. Ever since he got his license, he has been driving his dad's truck everywhere. It is nice to have a man with a vehicle and not have to rely on anyone else.

"Wow, you look beautiful. Are you ready?" I smile at him and grab his arm and then we are off for our first date in weeks.

One More Race

Jackson

This whole school year went by in a blink of an eye. I think it was because I was so damn busy with work and school. I tried my best to fit Taylor into my busy schedule to make sure she knew I didn't forget about her, but damn was that hard. I have been working so much overtime to try to save as much money as I can. One thing I can say is that Taylor has stuck by myside through the whole thing. I didn't think she would up and leave because our lives got busy, but I know that others probably would have. She's so patient when it comes to us, and it makes me love her more. I can't believe that we have been together this long already, I makes me think of our future when we will be looking back decades from now laughing at how we thought a year was a long time.

This year for race season has been fun. Taylor is still doing go karts, but I took over my dad's car and Andy has been racing on asphalt tracks like he said he was going to. He's damn good at it to. I'm still learning the ropes of being out on the bigger track, but I absolutely love it. I have raced a few times with Sam, and It was the best races I've done. Taylor still comes to all the races to watch to me, and Andy is there most of the time too. It great that we have all stuck together through everything. I think Andy is playing around with the idea of getting with Bethany. We joke around with him

One More Race

about it, but he never admits to liking her more than a friend, but time will tell with those two.

After this year I'll have my senior year and then ill be done with school and Taylor and I can start focusing on our garage. She tells me so much about school and it makes me so happy that she is loving her classes. I'm so proud of her for being able to take that number of classes and ace then on top of going to Boces with me. We have been working side by side to get our certification. It works out in our favor since its during the school day and I usually work on the weekends and sometimes the afternoons.

There is only one other girl in our Boces group and most of the guys single the girls out, but Taylor put a stop to it early on and I couldn't help but laugh. One of the popular kids from my school decided to go on a rant about how girls don't really know what they are doing under a hood of a car. I could feel the steam coming out of Taylors ears when this kid was talking, but before I could stick up for her and Marissa, she was on the kid. She challenged him with a damn engine build. He laughed at her, but I could tell that Marissa thought she was her hero that day. Of course, Taylor beat him and then continued to go on and tell him what he had done wrong just to rub it in his face.

    Not one guy said a bad word about the girls after that. Taylor tells me all the time about the sexism that comes to jobs and hobbies. I never really looked into it until I say it with my own eyes. Women really do get treated differently when they try to do a "mans sport." I'm just proud that my girl

One More Race

has the guts to stick to her goals and works damn hard to achieve them.

Alycia Carosella

One year Later

I still can't believe that I'm sitting here graduating at the same time as Jackson is. We both decided to meet up afterwards since our ceremonies were both at the same time. Funny how things like that happen, I graduated a year early and now we can't be together for one of the biggest accomplishments of our life. We both got our certification for Auto body and now we just need to get the funds for the garage and most of our dreams will be coming true. I got really good at photography in school and now

One More Race

I'm doing freelance which doesn't pay too much, but it makes me happy.

After the ceremony, my parents and Chris are taking Jackson and I out for dinner and I just can't wait to see Jack. Then Later he said he had a surprise for me, he isn't too good with keeping things from me but somehow, he has kept this one from me. As soon as I see Jack, I run up to him and wrap my arms around him.

"Hey sweetheart." He plants a kiss on the top of my head and then I turn my head up to face him. I go up on my toes to reach his lips and give him a kiss that tells him how much I've missed him. After years of being together, I still can't get enough of him, and I still lose myself in those Ocean eyes of his.

He always tells me that he wants our kids to have my eyes, but I wouldn't complain if at least one of our kids has his eyes. We talk about our future so much and it finally feels right when I picture mine in my head and Jackson is right beside me. We take our seats next to our parents and order our dinner without letting go of each other's hands. After dinner is done, we give our parents hugs goodbye, but my dad is smiling like he knows something is up.

"What's so funny old man?"

"Oh nothing, nothing at all."

I could sense that he knew something. Most of the time he always knew the secrets. I'll get it out of him eventually, but right now I just really want to know what my surprise is from Jack. We head out to his truck and as soon as he starts the engine, I start to question him about my surprise. I don't let

One More Race

up on him until I realize he is heading back to my house.

"Jack, where are we going?"

"You will see sweetheart." I hate surprises so much; I'd rather just know what it is. When he pulls into my driveway, my parents and Chris are there hanging outside. I knew it was weird with the way Jackson took here. He took the long way so I wouldn't see their trucks.

"Okay what's going on you guys?" My mother is the first to speak.

"We couldn't miss seeing your reaction." I turn to Jackson, and he has nothing but a smile on his face right now.

"Go open the garage sweetheart." I let go of his hand and made my way to the garage door. I slowly start to pull it open and that's when I see my surprise. I can't fucking believe my eyes; I can't believe it's mine.

"No fucking way!"

"Taylor Nicole Martin, you may be turning eighteen in a few months, but you need to watch your language."

"Sorry mom."

"Jackson, Is this mine? Is this the surprise?"

"I've been saving every penny I got from working and that's why I've been picking up extra shifts. I know it's not the best shape, but we can make her beautiful just like you."

I can't hold back my tears any longer. I let them fall down my face and I ran and jumped into his arms.

"I love you Jackson Dominic Ford"

"I love you Taylor Nicole Martin."

Jackson

Seeing Taylor's face after she opened that garage door and saw her race car made all that work worth it. I knew I was going to get her one as soon as she told me it was her dream car. I didn't realize how expensive those fuckers were though. So, I worked so much overtime to get enough to get her one, I got a good deal on the one I bought for her, thanks to Andy. I was nervous that she wouldn't like it at first, but it's us, we rarely got anything that was new, and we always appreciate what we had anyways. I think it was one of the things that brought us together.

Tonight, isn't over yet for us and I can't wait to give Taylor her other surprise. We spent the rest of the night in the garage. All of us together smiling and laughing like a family should be. The Martins have always felt like a second family to mine, and I can't wait to bring Taylor into my family. To finally intertwine them for real!

When it finally got dark enough out, I grabbed Taylor and got her into my pickup. I drove us out to the field a couple of miles away from her place.

"What are we doing here Jack?"

"You will see sweetheart." I got out of the truck and went around to open Taylor's door. When I went to the back of the truck, I rolled up the cover on my bed and Taylor's eyes got wide with realization. I

One More Race

had filled the whole bed of the truck with blankets and pillows.

There was supposed to be a full moon tonight and the sky was beautiful tonight. Never as beautiful as my Taylor, nothing in this entire world is as beautiful as my girl.

"Oh my god Jack! You're too good to me!"

"That's not possible. You deserve the world baby!" Taylor goes on her toes to kiss me, and I lift her legs around my body and climb into the back of the truck. I lay us down softly and continue to kiss her, in all the spots that I love.

"You're so damn beautiful Taylor, I can't wait to spend the rest of my life with you." She looks at me with her rainbow eyes and in that moment like so many before I can see our whole future together. Her being my wife, us working in the garage together, all our children that look just as beautiful as her running around our house. We slowly take our time taking each other's clothes off and memorizing each other's bodies. And I slowly make love to the women I'm going to spend the rest of my life with.

"Oh my god Jack, it's crazy how it feels just like the first time every time we do that." I smile at her and tuck the stray hair that was sticking to her sweaty forehead behind her ear. I can't help but think of our first time in her room after her mother had gone to sleep. We went inside to watch a movie, we fully intended on watching the movie, but I think we made it fifteen minutes and then we just knew that tonight was going to be the night. After the camp incident we wanted to make sure we were ready when the time came, and I couldn't have had a more perfect first time than I did that night.

Taylor was my first everything and it made everything feel that much better knowing that we were teaching each other what we liked. Over time we have gotten better with knowing what the other likes, what's the saying, practice makes perfect!

"It really is a beautiful night out; I wish I had my camera with me to take picture of that moon." I smile at her and get my naked ass up and reach through the back window of the truck. Her smile makes my heart jump, and I don't think that reaction will ever dim with her.

"Jackson Ford, will you marry me?" She is laughing and so am I when we come back together and press out naked bodies together. She snaps pictures of the sky and then turns to me. She gets on top of me and points the camera at my face.

"Smile Mr. Ford!"

"How could I not be with you on top of me like that." I grab her and flip her back onto her back and she squeals and laughs. I grab the camera from her and take a few shots of her. I take a few more pictures together before I can feel myself stiffen again and I think she takes that as a sign.

"Round two?" I turn towards her so fast I swear I break my neck. I take her in my arms, and we go for round two.

One More Race

Taylor

This past month has been a dream. Jackson and I have been working on my sprint car to get it ready for the races. Jackson has been racing his dad's old car since last summer and I finally get to be out on the big track with him this year. Of course, we won't be able to race together since we aren't in the same class, but we will be together afterward. We are currently loading the haulers up and going to head to the track. Jackson and I are going to pull my car and my dad and Chris are going to pull Jackson's.

    I hop in Jackson's truck and claim the radio for our drive. He usually never objects when I control the music. He hops in and gives me a huge smile and a peck on the cheek. The joker by the Steve miller band comes on and he looks at me and we both start singing to the song. Right after it says some people call me Maurice, he makes the sexy sound, and I can't help but blush because he is so damn cute. When he does little things like sing along to songs with me or big gestures like buy me a damn race car.

    I'm the luckiest girl in the whole damn world to be able to say Jackson Ford is my forever. Sometimes I get close to just proposing to him because I don't want to wait any longer to be able to call him my husband. When we finally get to the track, I start to feel nauseous, I don't know if I'm just nervous or if I'm actually coming down with something.

As soon as we park, I open the door and throw up. Jackson runs around the truck to help me out and helps me clean myself up.

"Are you all right sweetheart? Are you feeling sick?"

"I don't know, I think I'm just nervous for my first race" he takes my face in his hands and puts his forehead on mine.

"You will do just fine sweetheart, don't worry about it. Just go out there and have fun!" I smile and wrap my arms around Jack and give him the biggest kiss even though I probably smell like vomit. He must not mind though because he doesn't back away from me.

We unload the cars and get ready for the heat laps. Jackson goes out first and even though I've watched him multiple times out there on the track, my heart always races worrying about him. I know why my mother doesn't like being here unless she has to now. Watching it from home and being here are two completely different things. I worry about Jack crashing all the time and the first time he did I swear I about died, but then he got out and he was fine. The car on the other hand needed a lot of work, but we got it fixed and he was right back out there the next week.

Watching him out there on the track makes me so happy, to know that we did it, that we are still doing it. We are accomplishing one goal at a time together. When he comes back into the pits, he immediately starts getting me ready. I go out after the current cars out on the track now. I've test driven the car a million times since we have finished it, but this is real. I'm finally going to be out on the track with other drivers. My adrenaline is through the roof, and I can feel my cheeks hurting from smiling so much.

"Alright are you ready?"

"I think so." I say it with so much confidence I actually believe myself. Jack kisses me and then puts my helmet on. He is leaning against the car still in his fire suit when we put the steering wheel on. "Good luck sweetheart and have fun!" He taps the top of my helmet, and he mouths I love you to me and I kiss my two fingers and point them in his direction. Then I'm off on the track for the first time.

One More Race

Jackson

Watching her race on the track in the car I got for her fills me with pride. The smile on her face when she was inside that race car was priceless. That was how I was supposed to make her feel... happy! I watch her go around and pass cars and she is giving it her all. She is doing so damn good too, she definitely isn't letting up on the gas at all with the way she's drifting through the corners. Not once did she falter though, she stuck to her line and finished in third place.

"Good job sweetheart!" I grab the helmet from her, and I can see her eyes still light up from the experience. Our dads are here now giving us both hugs and telling us how we could improve on the track. I'm grateful for both of them still being here, I know they would rather be behind the wheel. My dad had to give up racing after back surgery, but he said he planned to retire after I graduated anyway because he wanted me to have his car. Sam hasn't retired yet, but he is more focused on Taylor and her racing. He's such a great dad and I'm so happy that he approves of me and Taylor.

After the features I plan to propose to Taylor, and I don't think she has any idea yet. I was originally going to do it the night I took her out in my truck, but we were a little preoccupied. I'm just hoping she likes it, now is the time to win the race for her so I can do it out on the track.

Taylor makes her way over to me and gives me a kiss. We look over the cars together to make sure we are set for the feature. She tells me everything about being on the track, how the car rode, what she thinks we need to tweak, how excited she is to go back out. I have no doubt that we both are exactly where we are meant to be. Here on the track with each other by our sides, we are a team. After we watch the rest of the heats, it's time for me to go back out and win this damn race for my girl.

I pull out on the track, and I push myself harder than I ever have before. I stick to my line; I look for openings and pass as soon as they open. I

Alycia Carosella

stay in third for most of the race and then I see an opening and I take it, I'm in second when the white flag goes out. I gun it and I'm catching up to first, we are side by side in turn four and we keep pulling back and forth. I'm on the outside and I start to lose the push but by some miracle I pass by just a smidge. I fucking won my race!

I pull on the victory lane and I see Taylor and our dads running down to congratulate me. I can't help but smile so damn big when Taylor jumps on me and kisses me so hard. We all posed for pictures and then the announcer came over to ask me some questions. I answer all his questions and then he asks who is like to thank for the win. I turn to my family.

"I'd like to thank my dad, Chris; without you I wouldn't have a car. Thank you to Sam for always

One More Race

letting us use the garage. Lastly thank you to my fiancé Taylor for always pushing me to achieve my goals" I can see Taylor go stiff when I call her my fiancé, I grab her hand, get on one knee and then lean into the mic again.

"Well technically she's not my fiancé yet." I hear the whole stands cheering at us.

"Taylor Nicole Martin, you are my best friend and I've always loved you from the moment I saw those rainbow eyes. I have no doubt in my heart that I will love you till my last breath. Will you make me the happiest man in the world and be my wife."

I'm surprised I was able to get through the whole thing because it could tell Taylor was itching to just say yes as soon as I got down on one knee.

"Yes Jackson! Of course, yes!" I scoop her up and spin her around and place the ring on her finger.

Alycia Carosella

The stands are wild now with all the cheering. I grab the mic before we leave.

"Now if you'll excuse us, I have to go get my fiancé ready for her race. Thank you."

The announcer goes on to talk about the proposal and how opening night just couldn't get any better than that.

We make our way back to the haulers to get Taylor ready for her race next!

One More Race

Taylor

Holy shit! I'm engaged to Jackson Ford! I can't believe he finally asked me to marry him. I can't wait to spend the rest of my life with this man. The whole way back to the haulers I couldn't help but look and my ring. I turn to my dad, and he had the biggest smile on his face. I hold up my hand to show my ring.

"Did you know he was going to ask?" He smiles and nods

"He came to me last week asking if he could ask you."

"He asked for your approval?"

"Yes, of course I was going to tell him yes. You have loved each other since as long as I can remember."

I give my father a hug and start getting ready to go out for my feature. Jackson pulls into his spot and hops out and runs over to me before I get into the car. He lifts me up and kisses me a million times. I can't help but laugh at his outburst of affection.

"You go out there and give them hell future Mrs. Ford." I kiss him and run my hand through his sandy blonde hair.

"I love you so much Jackson"

One More Race

"I love you to sweetheart." He gives me one last kiss before putting my helmet on and going out on the track.

I ended up finishing five in the feature which isn't too bad. I was in third for a while but towards the end I dropped back a little. I wasn't bummed though; I was still on my high of Jackson. Once we had gotten everything packed up, I went over to Jackson's house for the night. We made love four times that night and oh my god was it good.

When we finally fell asleep, I was wrapped in Jackson's arms, and I wished I could be like that every night. I remember telling him we should move in together, but it was two in the morning so I don't know if he would remember telling me that he had already gotten us a place. Probably another one

Alycia Carosella

of his surprises that he so desperately likes to do even though I tell him I hate them.

I secretly love them but only when they are from him. I'm hoping he mentions it today when he wakes up. Sitting here still wrapped into his arms and watching him sleep is the most peaceful thing on this planet. I can't believe I get to spend eternity with this man, marry this man, make babies with this man.

One More Race

Jackson

These past two months have been a dream. We moved into our place officially last week. I think we have christened every room at this point. We also set a date for our wedding, next fall. Taylor is so happy; I couldn't ask for a better life. This weekend is the biggest race of the season, and we can't wait to get out on the track again. We took the last weekend off to finish moving.

"Good morning sweetheart, I made fresh coffee."

"Good morning, Babe and thank you. I'm going to need it." I wink at her because I know why she is so tired. I am too but I'm too damn excited for tonight. I wrap my arms around her in her silk robe and grab the strap around it, pulling it to undo it.

"Maybe we can do one more race before tonight."

"It's not really a race when we both make it last for hours Jack." She runs her hand down my chest and stops when her hand is on my erection. She smiles at me and that's all I need before I'm picking her up and putting her back in our bed for round, I don't even know. She squeals when I drop her on the bed and come down over top of her.

We do not make love; we fuck, and God does it feel good. We explored each other in so many ways but it never feels boring with Taylor. It's like the first time even after all this time. Sometimes I wonder if it will be different after we are married

One More Race

but then we have sex, and it feels like this, and I know it won't.

We spend majority of the day in the garage getting the cars ready and loading the spare tires and tools in the hauler. Our dads got us a big enough hauler for both cars, instead of taking separate trucks every weekend. Our Dads go to every race with us, and Julia even came to two of our races. After the last one she went to, she said it was enough for her. Taylor ended up crashing into another car and she had freaked out. I would be lying if I said I didn't either, but she got out of the car with just a few bruises. I nursed her back to health and she was back out there the next week.

That's just part of the racing lifestyle, part of the thriller of beings out there. I head back to the house when Taylor has been inside for a good twenty minutes. She said she had to run to the bathroom before we loaded her car in. It doesn't take twenty minutes for her to even poop so I'm not sure what is taking so long. I go to the bathroom and see her slumped over the toilet throwing up. She hadn't done that since the very first time she had raced. Sometimes she lets her nerves get the best of her. I walk over to her with a wet rag and start rubbing her back.

"You okay sweetheart?"

"I don't feel so well, I can't believe I'm saying this, but I don't think I should race tonight." I'm shocked at her response; she must really not be feeling well. I scoop her up and bring her to the couch with a blanket and make her some tea.

"We don't have to go tonight sweetheart; we can stay home and relax if you want."

One More Race

"No Jackson. You've been wanting to go to these races for the whole season. I'll be right in the pits cheering you on. I feel a little better now that I've relaxed some."

"Have I ever told you how much I love you?"

"Every day Honey." I grab her tea and put it on the coffee table and uncover her. I tell Alexa to put on Josh turner and I grab Taylor and pull her close to me. Your man by Josh turner comes on and I start to sway with my girl in my arms in our living room. When he sings the opening line, I sing along to Taylor, and she starts to laugh at me while we dance. After the song finishes, I tuck her hair behind her ear and kiss her. We stare into each other's eyes until she realizes that time.

"We need to get going if you want to get a good spot. It's going to be packed tonight."

Alycia Carosella

I kiss the top of her head and tell her to relax while I finish packing the rest of the things in the hauler and truck. I leave her car in the garage and then we are off to the track. Maybe I can win this race tonight too, the prize money is more than enough to get our garage up and running. It could be another thing to cross off my list of things that make Taylor happy.

    I hold her hand for the whole ride to the track while we sing along to our music. Taylor is videotaping me singing to her and the way her eyes light up when I do it is the whole reason I keep doing it. I know I'm an awful singer, but I'll do anything to make her happy, that's what a partner's job is, isn't it? Taylor is my partner and always will be till the day I die.

One More Race

I wake up every day hoping she isn't a dream. Every morning when I wake up and roll over to see her beautiful freckles face and her sunshine hair, I have to reach out to touch her to just make sure she's real. Then when she opens those eyes, God her eyes have to be the best part of her. I hope our kids have her eyes!

Alycia Carosella

Taylor

This man has to be the sweetest man I've ever met, and I've got to be the luckiest girl on this planet to be able to call him mine. I always thought I would marry this man, but only because of our marriage pact. He makes me believe that soulmates are real because I can't picture my life with anyone else. When he sings to me, I can't help but smile, he's an awful singer but I won't ever tell him that. My heart swells so much with every little thing he does for me. Dancing in our living room will be one of my favorite memories together that we will tell our grandkids someday. I have so many stories to tell them already about how I fell in love with Jackson Dominic Ford.

We arrive at the track right on time and as I suspected, it's packed. We find a spot and start to get everything unpacked for the race. Our parents show up ten minutes later after everything is unloaded of course. Sometimes I think they do it on purpose, but they had helped us all throughout our first years of racing, so I don't blame them for wanting to come and just enjoy the races. My dad scans the area looking for my car and then looks at me confused.

"Where's your car Taylor?"

Alycia Carosella

"I'm not feeling one hundred percent today, so I told Jackson to leave it home." I can see his eyebrows raise and shock wash over his face. I can't help but laugh because that's the same look Jackson had when I told him I wasn't going to race tonight. I go out to have fun and I know I wouldn't if I felt like I was going to be sick in the car.

"Are you feeling better now? You should have stayed home and rested, honey." I laugh because Jackson and him are so much alike in ways and I couldn't be more grateful for that.

"Dad, I'm fine. I'm just going to help Jackson and watch the races." He kissed me on my forehead and smiled down at me. He made his way over to Jackson and Chris to do a once over on the car before the heats started. Sitting back and watching the three most important men in my life working on the race car makes me feel so full. My life couldn't get any better than it is right now.

    Jackson finished fifth in his heat and did so good for the number of cars there are tonight. It's going to be hard to stay in the front of the pack tonight. They split the heats into two parts because of the number of cars, but they will all be together for the feature race.

"You did so good out there babe!" I grab his helmet and give him a kiss.

"Tonight's feature is going to be rough." He grabs his helmet from me and sets it in his seat and wraps his arms around me. He kisses me on the top of my head, and I take in his smell that's wrapped around me. He smells just like the garage; he smells like home!

Alycia Carosella

"How are you feeling sweetheart?" I look up into his ocean eyes and smile.

"A little better, I'm still nauseous but not as bad."

"Maybe you're pregnant." He starts laughing but it gets me thinking. *When was my last period?* I haven't been on birth control for a few months because it was screwing up my hormones too much, but I've been tracking my period religiously since.

Jackson gets serious after he sees my hesitation and that I'm deep in thought.

"Are you pregnant Taylor?" He looks both nervous and hopeful in his eyes right now.

"Honestly, there's a possibility. Maybe, I can't remember my last period. We have been so busy moving that it slipped my mind." He picks me up and twirls me around like he's excited. He slowly lowers me to the ground and places his hand on my stomach and smiles at me.

"Jackson, we don't even know if I am yet."

"I hope you are!" His response shocks me a bit, but I wouldn't care if I was pregnant. We have always wanted kids and even though we wouldn't have planned it, I still wouldn't regret it. I never regret anything with Jackson, I smile and kiss his lips.

"Me too!"

We make our way towards the track, and I start taking pictures of the cars. I've gotten a lot better throughout high school and now with my photography. I always try to get pictures of Jackson's car in action, and I think I do fairly good. We shouldn't have any problems when it comes to advertising for the work we do on the cars for the garage in the future. I even helped Macy with some of her photography assignments. Thankfully, we still keep in touch after I graduated and moved in with Jackson.

We see Andy sometimes at the races, but we aren't as close as we used to be. I understand though, he's been going steady with Bethany for a few years now and he seems so happy. It's crazy to look back on our life's and then see where we are now.

It's finally time for the features so we make our way back to the hauler and get Jackson ready to go out.

One More Race

Jackson

Watching Taylor with her camera makes my heart fill with happiness. I know she loves to be behind the wheel of the car, but she is so good at capturing those special moments when you're behind the wheel and giving it your all. I can't believe she might be pregnant right now! It explains how she has been feeling the past week. I hope she is she will be the best mother there is, I have no doubt at all about that. I've always known I wanted to be a father and I'll forever be grateful to her for giving me that. As soon as we finish this race, we are going straight to get a test.

Back at the hauler Taylor helps me get everything ready and then I'm on the track. I start towards the middle of the pack so it's going to take some time to make my way up to the front. The green flag is out, and we all gun it. Right off the jump I gain two spots and I'm making my way up. I must hit a rut going into turn one because I spin out and then within a second another car clips my back end and spins out. I didn't see at first that the car that hit me had gotten hit as well.

The yellow flag goes out and the track officials make their way over to us. I wave them off letting them know I'm okay and make my way to the pits. When I arrive back at our spot everyone is there waiting for me. I see the worry on Taylor's face as soon as I lift the visor on my helmet.

"I'm fine sweetheart!" I see her expression soften when I say that. I point to the back end of the car where I got hit. Sam takes the piece that was hanging and rips it off. Nothing else seems to be wrong with the car so I should be able to go back out and finish the race. I look at Taylor and give her a smile even though she can't really see it through my helmet, but I know she can see it in my eyes.

"I love you Taylor Ford" she giggles when I use my last name instead of hers.

"I love you, Jackson Ford. Go kick some ass but be careful!" I put my two fingers to my helmet where my mouth is and then raise them in her direction. She kisses her two fingers and does the same. Then I'm back out just in time. They just finished

Alycia Carosella

cleaning up the track but now I have to start from the back of the pack. As soon as that green flag is out, I go for it!

One More Race

Taylor

I don't think I'll ever get used to the crashes. It's different watching when it's someone you don't know, but when it's someone you love it's unbearable. Thankfully, he is okay, and we were able to get the car back out on the track for him to finish the race. The green flag goes out and Jackson jumps up three spots immediately. He gains his spot back to the middle of the pack within a few laps. I see that he is struggling with finding an opening to gain more spots, but he rides it out.

Alycia Carosella

I'm standing with Chris and my dad watching Jackson race, my eyes are glued to him. One of the cars in front of him hits the wall going into turn one right in front of me and I hardly register everything that happens next. My heart stops as soon as I see the next car crash and then the two other cars. I try to see Jackson's car, but I can't see it through all the dirt in the air. I start to panic and then I see it, when he swerved to try to avoid the crash but didn't see the other car that he was about to run into. I yell to him even though I know he can't hear me.

"Jackson! "

He clips that car going so fast that he is airborne then his car lands upside down and slides into the wall. I clench my shirt because he has never had an accident this bad. I can feel the panic all around me coming off of the people around us. My heart fell out of my chest cavity and into my stomach when I heard the impact of his car into the wall.

"No! No! Please be okay, please God!" The track officials are on the track as soon as they can be and are helping the drivers get out of their cars. The other cars that weren't involved in the pile up are stopped on the track waiting to see if the drivers are alright.

"He's alright, he's got to be alright! Right?" I didn't realize I had said that out loud until I felt my dad's arms around me hugging me. I can feel the wetness of my tears strolling down my face. Chris is by my side clenching his shirt waiting to see his son step out of that car.

"Why isn't anybody over there? Someone get to him! Help him!" I'm screaming at everyone at this point to just help Jackson. The paramedics start pulling drivers out of their cars and when they finally get to Jackson's car, they try to lift the car up enough to see him.

"Why hasn't he gotten out yet? He would have gotten out if he was okay!"

The tow truck helps flip his car over and the car is mangled, and the top is caved in. As soon as they get him out of the car he isn't moving. His arms are limp at his sides, and I can't take it anymore. I wiggle out of my dad's death grip and start to run towards the track. After I almost get to the track, I feel an arm around my waist pulling me back.

"No, get off of me! He needs help! I need to get to him."

"Jackson!!!…. please wake up… please!" I can sense everyone around me staring at me, but I don't care right now. I sink into my dad's hold and fall to the ground into a crying mess.

Next thing I know, Jackson is airlifted out of the speedway and my father is driving all of us to the hospital. I'm dreading seeing him like that, but I need to hear his voice again. To just tell me that he loves me one more time and let me know that everything is going to be all right.

The ride over to the hospital feels like it takes hours when in reality it's only a thirty-minute drive. I think I've gone into full denial at this point because I'm not crying anymore and just frozen in my seat. I haven't been able to look over at Chris yet because I'm scared at what I'll see.

We finally get to the hospital, and we all run to the front desk and tell her Jackson's name. I expect them to rush us to him but instead she tells us to take a seat and calls someone. I think that's when I knew I needed to brace myself, that he must be extremely hurt. All I could do is just keep thinking he will be fine like he always is. *I mean we were just dancing; we're getting married, I might have his child inside of me. He has to be fine!*

Then a tall guy in a white coat approaches us and introduces himself to us. He tells us that he was the one who was here when Jack arrived. He starts to explain his condition and then he places his hand on Chris's shoulder. The next words that come out of his mouth come out slurred, or maybe it was just me.

"We did everything we could." My heart is no longer in my stomach, it's completely shattered and turned to dust.

"No! He's fine, he's always fine. Let me see him, I'll show you!" The doctor looks at me with sympathy and I want to grab him and shake him. I feel my dad's hand on my shoulder.

"Honey, he's gone." I feel the build up behind my eyes again and I don't hold them back. I cry into my hands at the thought of him truly being gone. I don't know how to live my life without him in it, it was supposed to be me and him until the end!

"I can't…. I don't…. I-I love him, he can't just be gone!" I finally look at Chris and he is looking at me crying just as hard as I am.

"I know Taylor. I love him to." He takes me into his arms and hugs me while we both mourn the love of my life.

Alycia Carosella

Epilogue

Five years later

"Breakfast is ready! "I hear the little pads of feet making their way to the kitchen. As soon as I turn around and see what my son picked out to wear for his first day of school, I can't help but smile. He is sitting at the table in his dress up fire suit, stuffing pancakes into his mouth.

"JD, I told you to get dressed for school, mister."

He stops his pancake mid in the air and turns and smiles at me.

"I did get dressed mommy, you told me to pick out my favorite shirt."

"Baby that's not a shirt."

"Can I please wear this…. please."

One More Race

"That's for playing JD, not for school." I see his smile turn into a frown and it takes everything in me to not just give in to him right there. He tilts his head down and I go over to hug him.

"I want him to go with me, I'm scared." I'm confused about who he is talking about.

"You want who to go with you honey?"

"Daddy." My heart breaks every time he talks about Jackson. He's never met his father, but he is so much like Jack, it kills me.

"I know that baby, but he can't. We've gone over this, is that why you picked this out to where?" He nods his head and looks up at me with those sweet little eyes and I can't help but give in. I mean who really cares what you wear to school now. JD is only five, but he is such an intuitive little guy, and he asks about Jack so much. I tell him everything because I want him to know everything about the amazing man that stole my heart.

"You can wear it baby!"

"But remember, daddy is always with you, right here." I point to his heart, and he gives me his crooked smile. The same smile Jackson would give me when I made him laugh. God, I miss him so much, JD is so much like him, and it hurts to have to do this on my own.

I drop JD off at school and head to the only place I need to be right now. I pull in and take a deep breath and make my way to him. I sit down at Jackson's spot and lay down on the ground looking up at the sky.

"Hey, you, not much has changed since I last came, but you should have seen JD this morning. He wore his fire suit to school." I laugh because I can't help

One More Race

but think that Jackson is doing the same thing, wherever he is.

"He looks just like you Jackson, he has your hair, that crooked smile of yours, but he has my eyes. I guess you got your wish with that. His are bluer in his than mine and I think he gets that from you." I put my hand on his stone and traced his name.

"He's such a smart boy too, he knows all his numbers and letters. You would be so proud of him, Jack."

"Oh, and the garage is coming along to, Andy says that it should be open by the fall. He even is having me the head mechanic even though he paid for the whole damn thing. You would love it there, its not like my drawing but its still perfect!"

"I wish you were here to accomplish our dreams together; you're supposed to be here, just the two of us forever!" I sigh and kiss his headstone trying not to be sad.

Hours go by and I just sit with Jack and go through our pictures and videos with each other. Then it's time to go get JD from school. It's crazy to think that I'm a mom now, but I wouldn't change it for the world! As We are walking back to the car, I ask him how his day was.

"Did you have fun on your first day sweetie?" He has the biggest smile when he is telling me about his day.

"Everyone said they loved my shirt, mommy and I made so many new friends. I even drew a picture for daddy. Can we please give it to him?" I get him buckled into his seat and nod to his question.

"Of course, we can honey." I make the drive back to Jackson and instead of feeling sad when I come here, I get a sense of peace. It's like I can feel him with us still and even though he can't talk back to me, I know he is listening.

We make our way to Jackson's spot and JD takes his picture out of his backpack.

"I had my very first day of school today daddy! I made this picture for you; I hope you like it. My new teacher had us draw what we wanted to be when we grew up, I even wrote my name on the back all by myself." JD handed the paper to me and asked me to read it aloud. It took everything in me to not cry reading it.

"When I grow up, I want to be a race car driver just like my daddy!" I look down at the drawing he did of a race car with the number twenty-four on the side and see that he printed his name on the back of

Alycia Carosella

the paper. In blue crayon it says Jackson Dominic Ford.

The End

One More Race

Acknowledgements

I want to thank my husband, Austin, for pushing me to finish not only this story, but also my other work in progresses. For always picking up the slack around the house so I could finish writing for the day. Thank you for always believing in me and helping me achieve my dream!

All my friends at work who boosted my confidence when I didn't think I was good enough to finish this story.

My book Tok community for hyping me up to continue with this story. You are all amazing and this wouldn't have happened if it weren't for your encouragement.

Made in the USA
Monee, IL
28 June 2022